THE SEVEN-MINUTE DECISION

BY

PETER MARIN

The Seven-Minute Decision
Published: June 2024
Printed in the United States of America
ISBN: 979-8-218-45456-2

ALL RIGHTS RESERVED. Except as permitted under the U.S. Copyright Act of 1976, no part of this publication may be reproduced, distributed, or transmitted in any form or by any means, or stored in a database or retrieval system, without the prior written permission of Peter Marin.

This book was published with the assistance of The WriteLight Group.

Copyright © 2024 by Peter Marin

TABLE OF CONTENTS

Minute One.. 1

Minute Two 28

Minute Three 42

Minute Four 56

Minute Five 85

Minute Six 97

Minute Seven 109

Epilogue... 120

Minute One

A sharp pain woke me. As I got out of bed and to my feet, another more powerful shock of pain electrified me. I was dead before I hit the ground. I found myself looking down at what, at first glance, looked like a pile of laundry thrown on the floor to the side of the bed. With a great rush of fear, I realized that I was watching myself die. The strangest sensation of all came over me. No, not over me, more like *through* me—a sensation that completely enveloped me with a realization that my reaction of fear was false. It was merely a well-rehearsed and programmed human reaction that had no impact in this new space I found myself in. I immediately felt safe and in oddly familiar surroundings.

I caught myself laughing at how predictable this scene seemed—me floating above, viewing myself from this transitional state. So far, it was everything I'd expected of dying, except oddly, I still felt embodied. There was a shift in time, as what was happening below me slowed to nearly a halt, and in this new space I found myself in, time remained at a normal pace.

I watched as Kim, my love and partner of many years, and our grandson, came rushing to my side. She called for help from her sons, and as the oldest reached me, he pulled me to an open space and began CPR. Our grandson's three-year-old mind couldn't quite grasp what was happening, and he started crying and holding onto his grandma as she called 911.

My perception of physical awareness and feeling was waning, yet I could faintly feel the chest compressions. The sounds from the room also diminished as everything slowed down. Then, as if being filled by a force with an overpowering sense of empathy, I was overcome by the combined emotions of my dear Kim, our grandson, and their fear, frustration, anger, helplessness and more than anything, their love. I was about to burst with conflicting emotions, my being responsible for them feeling this way, yet I was overjoyed when experiencing their unguarded love from this visceral realm. Talk about seeing through someone else's eyes! I was about to scream, "I don't want to leave you! I love you too!" when a friendly and familiar voice warmly called my name. I instantly recognized the voice of my near life-long friend and trusted business associate who had suddenly died four years ago.

As I turned in the direction of Douglas' voice, everything around me became a cylinder of lights—warm to brilliantly bright bursts reminiscent of psychedelic experiences I'd had. Although unnatural, they seemed completely in place—oddly normal and welcoming. At the same time, my body, though still there, no longer felt resistance from stiffness or pain, even gravity. It was as if I moved simply by thinking. To move painlessly was monumental for me! I had been living with debilitating, chronic neck pain for nearly ten years. Spinal fusion surgery helped, as did physical therapy. A daily diet of opioids and a trusted heating pad teamed up to cut my pain in half. So, when I turned towards my old friend's voice, in spite of all the other fantastic distractions, I noticed the lack of pain and that my movements weren't restricted. I could turn my head!

With all this happening, my mind was about to explode, when standing before me on a sun-bleached wooden beach pier was Douglas. All six foot five of his lanky, relaxed and suntanned self, smiled broadly and asked, "Wild, huh?" Chuckling, he extended his arms, inviting me into an embrace.

Greater minds than mine have attempted to capture and describe the various elements and textures that await us during our transition. Even drawing upon my direct personal experience, putting it into words, no matter what or how many adjectives I use, at best, I'd only be able to give you a glimpse of a partial sense of the magnitude and oneness of all, of all of us, of all things.

"Wild?" I asked, somewhat incredulous. "Douglas, I'm dying here!" Being two old show business vets, we couldn't let the double entendre go by, and we enjoyed a quick laugh and a hug at this bizarre reunion.

"It's okay, Peter," Douglas said. "That's why I'm here. I'll get you through this… well, more like *we* will."

Everything on this plane was perfect. Distractingly so. We were on a wooden pier above the clearest tropical blue sea graced with large, lazy, billowy white clouds, drifting on a light, sweetly perfumed breeze. Douglas wasn't the sixty-nine-year-old slightly pear-shaped version of himself who had suddenly died four years ago. He was a healthy and handsome thirty-five-year-old strapping man portraying him at his finest. Like I said, it all seemed perfect, yet I was just as aware somehow of my existence and circumstances on the "Earth Plane." I was simultaneously in two separate realities, completely aware and present in both, yet limited to real-time interactions and thoughts in my transitional plane. My view of the frantic actions below to help revive me remained in super slow motion, and seemingly at a distance.

Douglas, serving as my guide, was, once again, a choice that for me was, well, perfect. As I broke from our hug, I anxiously asked, "How do I go back? Can you feel how much this is hurting them?"

We both could see the "Earth Plane" scene moving so slowly it appeared to be a photograph. Douglas had an impish grin as he viewed my concerned familial crowd around me. Looking away from them and then straight into my eyes, with a deadpan delivery, he said, "I'm disappointed in you."

"What?" I muttered.

"That's exactly the way I died... remember? I stood up and fell right over—gone-zo, baby, it's gin, game over! Couldn't you come up with something more original?"

By now, he'd worked himself into near hysterical laughter while I just looked at him and said again, "I'm dyin' here!" The putz just kept laughing, turned, walked and waved so that I'd follow him.

As I fell in step with Douglas, I quickly stole a glance at my earth-bound scene; no, more like I thought of it, and therefore was transported to that nearly frozen stress-filled zone. Yet once there, I realized that I was somehow in both places simultaneously; I heard Douglas' laughter, not our grandson's cries of fear and confusion. I felt the sun and warm tropical breeze on my painless and free moving body—not the chest compressions frantically being administered on my behalf. The sudden awareness that the empathetic connection I had with my family was fading caused me to stop following Douglas. When I stilled, so did my connection with my earth-bound existence. I closed my eyes and tried to conjure the vision back, but no luck. Opening them again to the perfect tropical beach was suddenly disturbing. What initially had somehow seemed so natural—like finding Douglas as my "after life" guide in a place that normally would be a paradise to me, was now really creepy. There I was, cut off from my painful yet loving human existence, thrust into a seemingly perfect afterlife in paradise... It was getting pretty suspicious. Being pragmatic, I also realized that it didn't matter. I didn't seem like I had choices here, so I went along for the ride.

Douglas's laughter gave way as he offered me a reassuring and knowing smile. "Does this mean I'm dead?" I nearly yelled.

"Not necessarily," he replied, still smiling.

"What's that mean?" I asked, getting angry and frustrated. "And what the fuck are you smili-oh, shi-oh! I probably shouldn't say shi-stuff like that!!!"

Douglas was pretty amused by my outburst and emphatically assured me that words "like that" carried no negative value here, only bad intent is viewed poorly, regardless of which words are used in its pursuit. "Swear away!" he joyously proclaimed, still with that silly grin on his face.

Douglas' smile changed to a caring look as he watched me reach out and steady myself on the pier's railing. I was shocked that Douglas had felt the same way when he transitioned. I was too confused and overwhelmed at the time to realize that I hadn't verbalized my thoughts and my feelings, yet Douglas had read them as clearly as if I had. I stiffened and again closed my eyes... hard this time, like after glancing at the sun; and when I opened them, Douglas' caring look now encompassed total understanding. Without saying a word, his voice rang out clearly in my head, letting me know that there was much to review. Much to see.

Everything sped up. I felt like I was losing my balance and again, I reached out for the railing for support. It steadied me. A picture of the universe formed in my mind. Off center, gently drawing in the rest of the expanse was a black hole. With a massive burst, I was hurtled towards this black hole in a tunnel of laser like lights; and then, nothing. No sensation. No sense of self, only Douglas' voice saying, "Now we can begin, Peter. You create everything. Here, on this plane, or should you choose to stay longer on the physical plane and conclude that life differently. Time to refresh your memory." Then total silence. My mind went blank.

I experienced complete sensory deprivation, just for a second, then an enormous elevation of consciousness—intellect and awareness accompanied the opening of my eyes, and a new dimension was revealed to me.

It reminded me of sitting in an impossibly dark theater. When I say, "opening my eyes," this is merely descriptive, as I was now feeling disembodied yet powerfully aware mentally. This abrupt shift from a physical-mental being to a mental-spiritual one was oddly welcoming and warm, like coming home after being away too long.

An expanded view of my life, from its beginning to now, was presented to us as it exploded onto a 360-degree "screen", a sphere or bubble that we were spinning within. This "highlight" reel, featuring impactful experiences and interactions, focused on my spiritual growth and awareness. This was presented and was received on a nonjudgmental platform. Not without emotion, as I was still tethered to my earthbound state, yet very rationally, as my reasoning abilities had expanded with my intellect. Mind you, my highlight reel covering nearly 67 years played before and around us simultaneously and in real time, yet, even with us discussing people, places or thoughts that came up, no time seemed to transpire. The entire initial review of my life took only seconds.

Judging from the changes on the ground, where I was receiving CPR from Kim's son Finn, who, luckily for me, is a physician's assistant, an ambulance had been called, and Finn's professional manner had calmed everyone down... except Matty, our grandson. I could hear him fainting calling, "Papa, papa" as his crying faded out.

I no longer knew what would come next—not after "time", as past and present folded in on itself, presenting itself at once, while allowing access to individual moments, days, months and years. No. I was way out of whatever I may have projected to come next. Of course, the concept of time as an illusion—past, present and future existing simultaneously—this, I was familiar with, and to experience it, even with that expanded mental capacity, was overwhelming.

My fantastic time journey also revealed my personal progression as a spiritual being while being housed in human form. So much could be seen from a position nearly devoid of judgment and ego on a platform where negative judgment was not a consideration. This certainly did not meet my expectations with my Catholic upbringing. Religion was something that I truly found worth studying, questioning, and by my late teenage years, discarding. Judgment was certainly an expectation. A primary one, at that! Yeah, I was in uncharted territory, and as if he knew it, right on cue, Douglas said, "It's easy to see from here how important it is to be kind, isn't it?"

"Kind?" My first thoughts went to patience or understanding. I was blown away by all I was experiencing—my transition, mind and spirit expansion, and my life review (what, no punishment?). Yet Douglas simply assumed that with all that was happening, I would see the importance of kindness throughout my lifetime. It was like taking my mind from 180 miles per hour down to ten in five breathtaking seconds. Maximum intensity to focused singularity. Kindness?

As its meaning expanded before me like a glorious sunrise, I immediately understood the depth and connectivity that acts of kindness bring. By extending kindness, we elevate naturally our spiritual well-being while also suppressing human tendencies to judge and involve our ego. My life review showed that as I aged, I became kinder and not so quick to judge, among other things. I was beginning to see the simplicity of it all. Kindness breeds feelings of helpfulness and connects to other positive emotions, setting the proper tone for open communication.

"When being kind, we feed the whole of us, because we are one," Douglas said. "When did you become Sir Douglas Buddha, Jr.?" I teased.

"When I decided to stay here," he replied.

"Don't listen to him, Peter, my boy!" the voice of another dear friend and business partner said from behind me. I was so excited to hear Bobby Roberts' voice; I spun around as quickly as possible, blurring my view as I did, to find Bobby sitting in a booth, waiting to have lunch with Douglas and me at one of my favorite restaurants in Hollywood, California—Martoni's. It was located 1/4th of a block north of Sunset Blvd on Cahuenga Blvd and was a popular show business hang out, as well as an excellent restaurant. They had the best Clams Casino in town. They were to die for! What? Too soon? Sorry, bad choice of words.

Bobby slid out from the booth with the grace and ease of the dancer he was when he began his stellar career, a career that spanned five plus decades producing hit records (*The Mama's and Papa's*), timeless movies (D*eath Wish, Death Wish 2*), and so much more. A true Hollywood icon. More importantly, he was my friend. He whispered as we hugged, "Doug's full of shit." Then he gently pushed me away to arms-length, holding me by my shoulders and looking me straight in my eyes. As if nothing else in the universe existed except us, he asked, "How are you, Peter, my boy?"

"Not too good, Bobby! I think I'm dying!"

Interrupting, he said, "Only if you listen to Douglas!" Bobby then gestured for Douglas to slide into the booth next to him so I would sit across from them. Not being able to suppress a smile, I leaned forward and told Bobby how happy I was to see him.

It had been a long time. Bobby "took a cab," which is an old show business phrase for dying, in 2005. We had been doing projects together since 1998, and this had become more than a working relationship. We became family. Bobby's death hit me harder than any other, before or since. Seeing him at Martini's, no less, was seemingly perfect. Toss in Douglas, even though these two seemed to be at odds with each other, and I was with two people I loved and trusted. Then, like magic, two orders of Clams Casino and four setups just appeared! Perfect.

"Who's joining us?" I asked. Bobby just shrugged his shoulders in casual dismissal of my question while Douglas got busy helping himself to the clams. Following Douglas' fine example, I scooped a few clams onto my plate and popped one into my mouth...

Aha! Maybe this was heaven after all. The taste was magnificent! Nothing before compared to the experience of deeply tasting each ingredient. My mouth seemed to embrace and allow this delicately seasoned treat to present each layer of flavor, slowly at first, then picking up tempo like a beautifully written score to a romantic scene. My "enhanced mental state," I now realized, carried over to my other senses. I was intuitively able to fully appreciate even the simplest of things. I recognized and silently welcomed my newfound ability.

As I watched my two friends casually fill their plates, I suppressed a smile, and I mentally compared my "transition" and the subsequent "heightened senses" to becoming a vampire. Then Bobby wordlessly telegraphed to me, "Vampire's don't eat."

"They would if they tried these Clams Casino!" a chuckling Douglas replied.

I couldn't help but wonder why Bobby thought Douglas would lead me astray. What possible motive could exist in heaven or purgatory or wherever the hell we were for Douglas, or Bobby for that matter, to mislead me?

"We can hear you, ya know? And yeah, Bobby, I was wondering the same thing!" Douglas continued.

Bobby sat back, smiled and began to explain that my first spiritual encounter, which included an idyllic tropical beach and my happy-go-lucky old friend, was designed broadly to conform with my idea of heaven's gate.

"Your 'life review', from a semi-nonjudgmental point of view, was just one viewpoint and only meant to give you a baseline, because there are judgments here. You will see those later. For now, we are here to help you choose. Not everyone gets a choice, you know. You are being given an opportunity, on the one hand, to come home, heal and reflect on a well-lived life. Or you may choose to stay earthbound and extend your experience there."

"That sounds crazy, Bobby! What are you talking about? And how is Douglas giving me a bum steer? I don't get it. God! These clams are great!"

As my heartfelt exclamation left my mouth in exultation of those clams, a pulse of warm amber light formed and quickly faded around us, saying or thinking into our minds a wildly cheerful and loving, "Thank you, thank you! They are wonderful, aren't they?" This took me completely off guard, and the look on my face surely showed it. My two pals both were laughing at my surprised reaction to whatever had just happened, making me all the more curious. It dawned on me that fear never entered my mind, though on earth it certainly would have. Yet here, the extraordinary seemed ordinary. Everything was possible here if you could conceive of it, understand it, and I certainly didn't understand what just happened. *Did I just meet God? Over clams casino?* This thought got me laughing, too. Being with my old pals felt really, really good. Both Douglas and Bobby were people I loved and trusted in my life and missed deeply since their deaths. Being with them was, to me, then and now, a little piece of heaven.

Douglas interrupted my thoughts and said, "Who else?"

"Don't start." Bobby jumped in as I threw my arms up in semi-mock protest to stop them while Bobby proceeded, "Peter, this level allows for illusion. It's used to teach, to provide comparative scenarios as to reach one's highest spiritual enlightenment. This is a gradual process. Illusion can be deceptive, too." As he said this, Bobby extended his arms, one to each of us, and magically menus appeared in his hands.

"Dinner anyone?"

"What, a little sleight of hand?" I said with a snort. "Come on!"

Bobby, with a grin, conjured up a delicious dinner that instantly appeared before the three of us.

"Nothing for God, Bobby?" I sarcastically asked, pointing to the empty plate.

"Why bother? It's all an illusion," he replied.

"Can I eat it anyway?" asked Douglas.

I think his love for food is what ultimately got him. Good old Douglas loved to eat, and eat he did.

I was still waiting for clarification on my "pulse of light buddy". I understood, I thought, the use of illusion. I also was able to appreciate that time was an illusion and was being manipulated to allow me this "visit." But who or what just stopped by?

With Douglas moaning louder in delight with each bite while Bobby casually continued explaining the deal to me, I was momentarily lost in the past; it seemed so similar to the many lunches and dinners we had shared together. Through my dreamy reminiscence, I heard Bobby say, "I was saying toys and trucks and cars..."

"Wait, what, Bobby?"

"I was saying," he answered, "that illusion and reality can be, to some, one and the same. When your beautiful three-year-old grandson plays with toys, trucks and cars, they are very real to him. His young mind will soon learn that that was an illusion, and he will outgrow it. Just as we did." As Bobby reached to the center of the table, a silver plate appeared full of what looked like the finest cocaine I'd ever seen, and I have seen more than I should have.

"You think the clams were good, try this!" he continued. As much as I once enjoyed that devil powder, now I couldn't care less, and I told them so.

Then, three of the most beautiful and elegant women sat in a booth across from us. We all took notice, as they were each exceptional. I turned to face the guys when Douglas said, "they're here for us, or all for you, Peter, if you want."

I was shocked! Bobby said, "Not for me." I added that I had quit coke and speed over twenty-five years ago, and, regarding women, since I learned what love is, no matter how pretty, sexy, or how many, the answer was no. "If my actions hurt the woman I love, I won't do it."

"But you're here, Peter, it's cool, man."

"No, Douglas," I said. "It's not! And where is here? Please stop with the tricks and temptations and tell me who that was in the amber light!"

In his typical calm and stately demeanor, Bobby quietly brought the conversation back to illusions.

"The drugs and the women at one point in your life would have pleased you, yet you've grown past those desires physically and emotionally. Here, and there," he paused, motioning with his head so we would see my earthbound scene, where, by the way, little had changed. "Being here, the relationship to our former human self is similar in that one no longer is dependent on such things or desirous of them. We certainly appreciate them, see and understand their value, their beauty or not. From here, you'll continue to love and communicate with those still embodied; your spirit will infuse them with your wisdom and knowledge at will, should they be open and willing to receive it. Peter, you are not dying. Should you choose to stay now, you would simply be releasing your spirit from its shell, to another form of existence. You see, we never die. We only change. It's as if there are layers of life and of living."

Douglas smiled ear to ear, pleased by his meal and Bobby's comment, and chimed in happily with a dramatic quote, "A change is gonna come!"

I smiled, more for me, shook my head gently and replied, "Maybe not today, guys. I'm loving being here with you, you have no idea. Yet this feels surreal, dreamlike, while that," I motioned to the view of my earthbound scene, "feels real."

Douglas interrupted me, "that's how it should feel because here, you ain't seen nothing yet!"

Bobby shrugged and replied sarcastically, "You are so eloquent, Douglas."

Douglas and Bobby hadn't known each other in their lifetimes; Douglas and I were together in our youth and Bobby and I later in our careers. As I watched them interact, I realized that my earlier impression that Bobby somehow thought Douglas would mislead me was incorrect. Bobby was just being himself and being protective of me and establishing control. I guess some things just don't change. As for Douglas, he took Bobby's moves and comments all in stride, also true to form. Douglas was always one cool customer. My thoughts drifted to the many times I'd had meetings and meals here at Martoni's, which lead to recalling how socially oriented and active my business life had been before I became sick in 2008, where I suffered severe memory loss and depression.

Lost in thought, I didn't notice the server approach us until he was tableside and addressing Bobby, saying, "Mr. Roberts, your last guest has arrived."

"Please bring him in," Bobby replied. As he said this, he stood and watched the server walk towards the entrance. We rose as well, anticipating finally meeting our mystery guest. The server opened the door, exposing a pure, extremely bright white light that back lit the scene, effectively presenting us with two approaching silhouettes. Once they were fifteen feet or so from us, one figure faded into the light as it retreated through the exit, revealing a very skeptical Mort Sahl.

The father of political satire and former speech writer for John F. Kennedy stood before us, and as soon as he saw us and recognized where he was, his skepticism shifted to sarcasm.

"Martoni's, Bobby! This isn't my idea of Heaven, man! This can't be right!"

Mort raised his arms and slowly circled them as he surveyed the joint in complete astonishment. When his gaze fell on Douglas and me, he half smiled and said, "Oh, hi Peter. I'm sorry, I'm just so…"

"That's fine, Mort," I interjected. "I really get it, I do! No need to apologize. And, Mort, meet my old friend, Douglas."

Mort, still somewhat distracted, shook Douglas' hand, while I motioned for both of them to sit in the booth.

Mort was impatient. As Douglas sat down, he stood there looking determined to find the same answers I was seeking, although he was going about it in his own, unique way. I already saw that his and my paths were not the same.

"Bobby, come on, what's going on here! This can't be the end of the line!" Mort nearly yelled.

Bobby's unique way of making you feel as if you were the only person in the universe was an amazing talent of his. Bobby applied this to bring Mort under control and calmly said, "Of course not, and we will get to that. I've been expecting you, Mort. Sit, please. I'm here to help you with all of this."

"HA!" Mort exclaimed.

"I knew things went terribly wrong when Trump got elected. Believe me, I felt like checking out right then. Bobby, this is blowing my mind. How deep, or maybe, how high, has the corporate power and corruption penetrated that my manager is required to negotiate my deal with heaven? And Bobby, that's the only deal I'll accept! A heavenly one! Anything short of that could have me spending eternity with someone like that crazy orange faced bast... well, you know. And that would be hell indeed!"

As we took our seats, Bobby asked Mort if he knew why he was here. Before replying, Mort scanned the room, again. He then looked meaningfully at each of us. Douglas, me, then lastly, Bobby. Douglas he had just met. I met Mort and Bobby in 1998, when Mort was booked to headline for a week at Basin Street West, a supper club I spearheaded in Rancho Mirage, CA. Bobby and Mort's relationship spanned a few decades; sometimes as manager-client, always as close friends.

While Mort took all of this in, he apparently had a revelation. His face lit up, his eyes widened, and he had a smile from ear-to-ear. He leaned slightly backward and extended his arms to the sky and proclaimed, "Yes! I know! I'm here because Bobby, since the day you died, I would tell people that you went ahead to canvas the market for me, to get things ready for me. Saying that, making light of you being gone, made it a little easier for me. I said or thought that so often, I suppose I came to believe it. That sound about right?"

Bobby smiled and looked at Mort with all the kindness and warmth you would expect of such close friends. "That's it, exactly!"

Mort's reaction to this was vintage Mort Sahl. "HA! I love you, Bobby, but this isn't my idea of heaven!"

"I get it, Mort, let's take a walk." Before Bobby and Mort left, Bobby turned and said goodbye to Douglas. To me, he gave a short hug and said, "However you decide, I'll be with you soon. By the way, Peter, you should be very proud of the recovery you've made. Great work, my boy."

We all said our farewells. Mort and Bobby opened the exit door, once again showing the bright white light outside, causing them to instantly become silhouettes. Suddenly, from outside, a third silhouette appeared. I heard Mort breathlessly exclaim, "Morty!" as the third figure cried "Dad!" and the two figures became one in a furious, emotional hug.

Mort and his only child, Mort Jr., who died at the age of nineteen in 1996 as the result of a drug interaction, were joyfully reunited. Mort Jr.'s death had left his father so hurt, so depressed, that the mere mention of his son, right to the end of his life, could bring Mort to tears.

As the door closed, we heard Mort say to Bobby, or to God, or to both, "Thank you, thank you."

"You okay? Hey, Peter!" Douglas was nearly shouting to get my attention. I was so absorbed in all that had just happened, my mind was blown. The elation Mort felt when being reunited with his son had washed over me as a display of love so pure, I stood there, paralyzed, basking in this radiant moment before I responded to Douglas.

"I'm fine. No, no, I'm not, Douglas. I'm… I don't know. That was amazing! When Mort connected with his son, I felt it! It was wonderful!"

This "place" where I found myself was truly magical. The expansive source of emotion and knowledge that was presented to me here was more appealing than my words can describe. Yet I found myself terribly conflicted.

Having been given the choice to pursue this spiritual existence or to reclaim my physical one presented a larger dilemma than one might imagine.

Rejoining my body would allow me to enjoy the most wonderful loving relationship and also would give me more time with our grandson. Yet I would also return to constant chronic neck pain, caused from a fall in 2012. Thinking of the pain is what caused me to pause, to consider making this a one-way trip. It's not just the pain to consider. The by-products: pain meds and their side effects, loss of physical abilities, and sometimes desires, etc. The culmination of these often result in feelings of isolation. Isolation, for one like me that lived an exceptionally social life, where business and friendships often were one and the same, resulted in depression. Fortunately for me, this is familiar territory. Not to say it isn't perilous at times, but I'm not the type of guy to check himself out. No suicide for me. It's not that the thought hasn't crossed my mind. I think I can understand, though, how one might make that decision. Sadly, I think too many may be driven out by depression. I do wish that they could have held on for one more hour, one more day, perhaps. It may have looked different, may have gotten better. To those with serious health issues, at some point, at *that* point, I get it. And I'm not that brave, I don't think. Plus, I couldn't imagine leaving Kim that way. She is the best friend and life partner to me imaginable. Suicide would dishonor everything good and honest between us.

During my thoughts, Douglas interjected, "What's the difference? Didn't you commit suicide? Did you exercise like the doctor told you to? Did you eat the right foods? Kim tried! She cooked proper foods and suggested exercising. Or did you lay around, eating crap and groaning about your pain, until you fell over dead? Semantics!"

"Wait one min—" I was cut off...

"Stop right there," Douglas said while smiling. "So I'm being harsh, so maybe it's not exactly suicide, but you get my point." I shook my head and smiled back at my old friend, relishing his folksy illogic.

"I've missed you, pal. You are truly one of a kind. You do know there's a difference between eating bad and putting a gun to your head, right?"

Douglas suddenly transformed into a warm, pulsating orange and yellow light form. His general shape was preserved, giving him somewhat of a physical presence. Our surroundings, a split second later, morphed into what looked like a welcoming sea of calmly interactive light forms of various hues that seemed to cradle and support me in the most secure and freeing way. Then the amber light, the light that spoke to me earlier, spoke again...

"The reason to stay is the same as the reason to go. The reason is always love."

Minute Two

The morning of what appeared to be my final day began normally. I woke up around four-thirty a.m., popped my first pain pill of the day, had coffee while I read the news and then headed into our home office to write for a few hours. At least that was my intention. I was working on my third book, my second novel. I was finding it difficult to focus and convey my thoughts, to translate them onto pages. More than anything, it seemed I found myself drifting in unrelated thoughts and losing time. I felt as if I was avoiding where my storyline was going because it cut too close to home. It touched a place in me that I didn't want touched.

"So, don't write it!" I'd tell myself and had been doing so for days now. "Change the direction of the story! Stop doing this to yourself! See a Doctor! Take a Xanax! Weave a basket! DO SOMETHING!" Let's just say it wasn't going so smoothly at that point. Yeah, a pretty typical start to the day.

Through my hazy fog of frustration, I heard the familiar jiggling of the office door handle, followed by one of my favorite sounds ever... our grandson Matty calling me. "Papa, Papa!" he proudly announced as he knocked on the door. "Papa, I'm awake, I'm awake!"

"Matty, so am I!" I replied as I opened the door to a smiling, three-and-a-half foot, curly blond-haired puckish imp that owns my heart. If he had a "mobster nickname", it would be "Little Matty Two Times," 'cause he always repeated everything twice. He extended his little arms up to me, saying, "Hi, Papa. Whatcha doin, watcha doin'?"

As I lifted him up for a good morning hug and kiss, I immediately felt my spirits lift, too.

"I'm playing trash trucks and reading books with you, that's what I'm doin'! What's first?"

"TRASH TRUCKS! TRASH TRUCKS!" he excitedly yelled, forgetting that everyone else in the house was still sleeping. Having been happily rescued from my temporary drudgery, off we went to rid the imaginary world of stinky, slimy, yucky trash! Vroom-Vroom… beeeppbeepbeep! Vroommm!

It wasn't too long before the smell of eggs and hash-browns filled the house as Kim, aka Momma, finished making breakfast for us. Her timing was perfect, as I was just about done filling and emptying and filling again the toy trash cans and trucks for the umpteenth time, not because I wasn't enjoying it; no, only because my neck was killing me. Yet our young Matty, full of health, youthful exuberance and endless imagination, never tired of it. He could play trash trucks for hours! If not for this damn neck of mine, I would, too! I loved spending time with him. I usually got the early morning shift, giving Kim and the uncles a chance to sleep in on a weekend morning.

Matty and I alternated through his top three favorite activities most every morning; playing trash trucks, reading books, and playing "thaxathpone, tombone, and tumpet," which are represented by small metal Christmas tree decorations of each. Recently, he showed a pointed interest in and talent for drumming, so Uncle Jayce (Santa) got him a

"Pocket Kit" for Christmas, which is a real, just small, drum kit... and Matty is killin' it (after everyone's awake). Man, do I love the morning routine!

Today, after breakfast, I tidied up the kitchen while Matty and Kim started their day together. You see, once Kim was in the scene, I took a backseat right away. Matty was pretty much attached to her at the hip. At this point, he was a Mamma's boy, 98%! Matty would follow Kim any and everywhere and be her "helper" in all things, needed or not. From the time he could walk, Kim put him to work. He loved to vacuum more than almost anything. He was so into it that Jayce, Kim's oldest son and Matty's favorite Uncle, bought him a miniature vacuum, identical to the house one. Hmmm, I wonder who had who wrapped around who's finger? He'd got us all wrapped up, that was for sure. And we couldn't be happier about it.

With Kim in the lead, the two of them went off to play, learn, go on adventures, clean up and then run errands. I went to the post office then returned to our office for a couple more hours of work for Kim's business, until I ran out of steam around eleven a.m. and went upstairs to pop another pain pill, lay down and watch the news. Next thing I knew, a friendly, cute little curly-haired alien creature was rousing me from a deep slumber, attacking me, jumping up and down on me, loudly and cheerfully quoting and acting out a favorite literary title of his. "Hop on Pop!" "Pop" was emphasized breathlessly while he landed on my waiting abs, or more like flabs. We tussled for a few minutes and played, and as quickly as he had appeared, he was gone. He ran out of the room, rounded the bedroom door and headed for the stairs, calling for his momma to start a new adventure. I checked the time, and four p.m. had come and gone. I had slept away another afternoon... so far, another typical day.

I straightened the pillows, turned off the news and sat up in bed. I thought how lucky we were to have Matty living with us, and how much I missed him lately at nap time. Sadly, for me, he had recently outgrown naps just as I was completing my Olympic level nap training, leaving me looking like a lazy 'ol slog instead of a loving and supportive grandpa. It also provided some changes for Kim.

Until a few months ago, Kim would use our afternoon naptime to work. She could get three or four hours of business done. Now that the little angel had outgrown them and wasn't snoozin' with Papa and seeing as he loved his Momma more than anything or anyone and must have her in sight, Kim was now working until three a.m. to make up for it. Now that's true love. Kindness and love.

These are the thoughts I was having as I was cradled in that amazing sea of comforting gentle pulsating light. The thoughts and doings of that day... the memories, the feelings.

For the most part, I was feeling grateful. I noticed that an old friend had called, and the thought that we'd been pals for forty-six of his ninety-four years made me feel even more grateful. So, I called him right back. He wasn't home. His voice message said he was joining friends for dinner. Good for him! Ninety-four and still raising hell! I made a note to call him the following day... (well, the odds are down on that right now).

Matty's drumming filled the house. I settled back into my pillows and listened to him hit his snare drum and tom-tom, then crash hard on a cymbal, then soft on the high-hat... then all hell broke loose! He was having a BLAST! And listening to him was wonderful...

I woke up with a nostalgic, almost reflective attitude. It seemed both like a lifetime ago and like yesterday when I suffered severe memory loss. I recalled the fight back. It was the love of family and friends and the power of music and passion that helped me every day. The healing and clearing that came with writing a book about my life and my recovery from memory loss, as difficult as that was (and man, was it!), would help a lot of people. I chuckled at myself at the many times I should have written myself off, said that I was through, whether it was professionally, personally, or socially. I came close. And while I was in this nostalgic review, with the drumming of "Matty Two-Times" (who just may be the next Ginger Baker or Louis Belson) in the background, I once again felt like one of the luckiest people I knew. And, by extension, our little Matty as well.

Matty had lived with us since his birth. Due to many complications: health, his parent's divorce, the pandemic, along with other issues, it became Matty and his parent's best interest that he lived with Kim and me as his legal guardians. The difficult decision on his parents' part, to do what was best for him, was working out wonderfully, well, except for Kim's sleep deprivation!

His birth parents, who moved out when Matty was four months old, visited rarely. They served in more of an "Aunt" and "Uncle" role, while two of his three uncles here at home were more like big brothers, with Jayce most like a father figure. He'd been surrounded by people that love him since day one, and it showed in his well-adjusted and curious, happy demeaner. That's why I thought he was one lucky little monster! And for the most part, it was because of Kim. Kim was our common denominator.

Again, I laughed at a time when I thought that I knew love was a myth; something only songs and plays were written about, or other people found. For me, it had been unattainable, something I made a few noble attempts at, yet never quite realized. I honestly thought those bells were ringing a few times and found out too soon it was more my youthful enthusiasm, lust and a twisted desire to conform. That allusive thing called love and I danced together many times, and it always seemed to go home (or stay forever) with someone else. Finally, being disillusioned with it, and otherwise distracted, I'd stopped pursuing relationships, even dating, for years until quite unexpectedly, Kim came into my life. I sat laughing at how silly it was to shut my mind to anything, to think that I'd reached the pinnacle of knowledge on whatever the particular subject, and again how fortunate I was that Kim proved me wrong. Spending a few minutes on daily reflection had become a form of centering for me. I didn't always approach my reality with the feelings of gratitude that I possessed now, and to be clear, those emotions still slipped on occasion. Ghandi I was not! Taking time to reflect on past situations, failures and successes in order to appreciate their contribution to my unusual, turbulent, talent-inspired, star-studded, magnificent life (that I wouldn't wish on anyone else) helped me to focus on how far I'd come since losing my memory, aiding me in maintaining a grateful outlook. I was, for far too long, caught in a mindset where I felt more defined by my limitations as opposed to my progress.

The ebb and flow of my ten plus year recovery process with my memory issues dovetailed into other challenges regularly faced by those of us nearing middle age and retirement, feeling useless. Not useless, more like "less-less." I'm kidding, mostly. It's common to find the changes we go through as we age challenging. I get it. Plus, for me, after eight years into coming ¾ back from nearly being a walking zombie, I was finally realizing some semblance of a "normal" life. I was singing with an excellent jazz band and starting to socialize again when I had an accident that transformed that proverbial light at the end of the tunnel into the headlight of a high-speed train! I fell and got a spinal injury, resulting in neck surgery. Sadly, I'd only enjoyed moderate pain relief from that surgery and the subsequent treatments.

A speeding train was coming right at me! Chugga, chugga, chugga, chugga, choo-Choo! Thankfully, not that time! If that light had been anything other than a symbol of Kim's belief in me, and if I hadn't had her to help me through that readjustment period, my path would have been a dark one, for sure. I feel grateful for the opportunity to experience love. And through that, to be able to appreciate the vast differences that exist in my abilities now versus then, and my lifestyle now versus then. There are and were many elements that I loved of my past, and once they were gone, it initially caused me to be depressed. I had some high, high times! And I mean that in as many ways as I can. I went through some changes and now I'm accepting more of the natural order of things, and I must give credit to that most basic of emotions that had eluded me most of my life—love.

I had to watch, too, so I walked downstairs to enjoy the concert. He beamed when he noticed me 'round the corner to fetch a front row seat to clap and cheer as he performed a drum solo with skill far beyond his age. "I think this kid's got talent," this proud Papa was thinking as he played, in time, while also singing "Old MacDonald" mostly in tune. He finished BIG, with cymbals crashing and bass drum pounding! It was something to behold. I responded with rousing applause! Kim ran in from the kitchen cheering her approval followed happily by our two barking dogs, who were jumping up at her and each other in all of the excitement. Matty was loving every minute of the attention, enjoying it with the enviable abandonment of a child. It was a beautiful moment! A star was born! A tear snuck out of my eye. I was so happy. Kim joined me on the sofa for a private snuggle. The dogs jumped on us followed by Matty, of course! In seconds, our sweet little cuddle turned into WWE! It was total chaos and hysterical fun. I wore out too quicky and, covered in dog and kid spit and slime, I headed for the shower.

My thoughts defined themselves to those of a more spiritual nature as the steamy water seemed to rinse away any trace of negative notions. It was from this perspective that I reviewed the last few years, the time that we'd had Matty with us. Stepping into the fogged-up shower almost seemed to transport me to the beginning of this new period in our lives, allowing me protection, somehow, from viewing what happened any other way than this way. Again, Ghandi, or Buddha, I'm not. I do not view myself as an exceptionally spiritually advanced person. Having been curious from a young age, I have studied these subjects and favor them, yet I am no expert.

During this very relaxing shower, I experienced a focus of positivity whereby all events had an equal value. Adjustments that had been "difficult" were not deemed as such, therefore given basically the same value as those activities that required little change. No bad, no good; just all with a positive slant. I even saw that "slant" in my son-in-law! It all made perfect sense, in theory, and could have dissipated with the steam as I stepped out of the opened shower door because I suddenly felt weak. I thought I was going to black out.

I grabbed the shower door to steady myself, which wasn't too smart, seeing as shower doors are on hinges and swing! Ahh, and the good news! I caught myself, mid swoop, looking like a drunk dancer trying to catch himself before a hysterical wipeout! What a scare, though. I wrapped up in a towel and sat on the edge of the tub to get my legs under me.

Still reminiscing in a spiritual mindset kept my near-mishap from altering my outlook, although I did register concern as to why all of that just happened. Just getting older, I supposed. Another malady to add to the ever-expanding list of challenges and ailments assigned to those of us fortunate enough to keep adding candles annually to the proverbial cake.

"Now wait a minute here, I'm too young for this stuff!" I rebelled to myself, and just as soon as I did, I answered myself right back, "Yeah, and you've burned the candle on both ends for most of your life! Are you really surprised?"

Sitting there, warming up under that thick, cotton towel and catching my breath, I had to admit that I wasn't that surprised. My past exercise and healthy diet routines are things of fantasy, although I do now take both subjects seriously. I stopped drinking hard liquor in 1991 on a bet that I couldn't stop for sixty days. I not only won the bet, but I also still do not drink to this day. After the required two-month period, I ordered my usual Vodka-rocks with a splash of water and a lemon twist. As I raised the much-anticipated drink to my anxious lips, the smell immediately turned my stomach. To this day, I just can't get past the smell. On occasion, I will enjoy a glass of wine or a cold beer on a hot day, but the hard stuff, not anymore. You see, I never had a drinking problem. I only drank to take the edge off the cocaine I was using. Which meant that I drank a lot. Thankfully, I also stopped all the drugs years ago—the coke and meth.

No, I wasn't surprised. And I certainly wasn't ready to let my sordid past catch up to me now. That would be the opposite of poetic justice, in my humble opinion. Here I was, finally sitting kinda pretty. I had the most wonderful woman and family. A beautiful grandson that filled my heart in a way that was different from any feeling that I'd ever known. The satisfaction I received when hearing from readers of my books telling me how my experiences had contributed positively to their lives, and how much fun I was having singing and "making music with my friends", as "good 'ol boy" Willy Nelson put it. Now that I'd had nearly twenty years of clean living, I was thinking it would be a lousy time to shut my show down. I shook off that thought, because I had a show of my own to get ready for…

Minute Three

Then I was suddenly aware of Douglas' presence, his aura, which brought my thoughts back to this moment. I was moved, and not startled by being transported once again into the cradle of lights that immediately felt familiar and safe. Having just been remembering my first true sense of being in love and being loved by Kim, of feeling so at home with someone that trust is a given, and being my imperfect self was not just ok, it was expected… the cradle of lights took my recollections and wrapped me with love and empathy, showing me the purity of my bond with Kim and Matty. Sharing these thoughts and sensations, Douglas nodded his understanding of my confusion. I was beginning to experience visions and sensations, heightened levels of awareness that were wonderful and perplexing. With heighted awareness I saw where and how I fit in to this fantastic universal picture, and as clarifying as it could be, it seemed to be equally confusing. I wanted to see more, so much more. I wanted to stay. I wanted to be with Kim. And Matty. I wanted to go.

I felt as if part of me was being absorbed into the lava-like flow of colorful, fluctuating lights which I was beginning to accept as God, or Source. It was not a singular entity; more of a collective, something different from the more popular teachings I've encountered, yet not an unfamiliar philosophy. Simultaneously, an emotional surge greater and more joyous than I had experienced prior drew me to my partner and grandson, as well as to the other people in my current life that I love. The mere fact that I could be confused by the choice between staying in this heavenly place or returning to complete whatever may remain of my physical existence on earth was, well, confusing. You'd think that it would be no contest, yet I was truly stuck in my personal Purgatory.

This paradox caused me to recall an isolated moment during my early education as a child in a Catholic school when a priest described Hell as being "outside the sight and presence of God." I didn't agree with too much of what the church was selling, even as a youngster, but I understood this concept. I suppose it was because my dad was away at sea most of the time, and that helped me relate to the "out of sight" concept equaling bad and lonely feelings.

Would I lose all of this if I didn't stay? I asked myself, or so I thought. Without realizing it or really having even thought of it, I had meshed with this Source in the way we communicated. It no longer seemed so much a dialogue between me and individuals, but rather a self-dialogue that somehow included the input of the whole. Communication was made more direct, simple, straight to the Source. Put simply, it was like talking to myself and answering myself with really great answers that I would never come up with on my own... yet those answers, those feelings and responses, would be so simple, you'd think I should have them! And the bubbling undercurrent of the light flow that surrounded and supported me somehow communicated to me the complexities that support the answers, which I absorbed through a process not unlike osmosis, presenting a mountain of evidence and research to verify the conclusion. It was all so strange and yet so natural at the same time.

"It will be different, of course," echoed back the distilled response. It was the "Of course" part of the response that got my ever-expanding mind to roll... to suddenly consider an emotion, a feeling that I thought I had all but forgotten. And the tone of the answer raised deep within me what I tend to believe is the true "Original Sin"; the curse shared by humanity—fear. *Fear, the insidious cancer that it can be, has no traction here,* I thought, fighting back the swelling pressure of it which I felt filling the space where my chest would be. "It is merely an echo of a deeply programmed response. There is nothing to fear. There is no fear. Yes, all will be changed, should you come later. Yet all will change momentarily, regardless. Change is constant on all planes, and in all thoughts. Here, there is nothing to fear."

The swirling mass of dancing lights reformed itself, still cupping me safely as it glided now towards a brighter area that glowed a soft orange and yellow. The sensation of motion ceased and a warm feeling of being in a spa or hot tub ensued. My view was elevated over a smooth amber and gold fluid (of which I somehow was part) past what looked like an eternity edge to the sea of pulsating lights. This time, my vantage point seemed to suggest that as expansive as what I was seeing was, I was not seeing everything. It was also obvious that the different colors throughout this dazzling array of lights must have meaning beyond their spirits, souls. My first thought was that there was a "caste" system, which immediately felt wrong! Voter suppression in Heaven!!! Unequal Pay in Paradise!!! Can ya see the headlines, folks?!

Fear and inequality. One I'm told doesn't exist here, and the other, I can't imagine could.

"Then why do I feel fearful of staying? Hell, of going back, for that matter! And I'm confused by the variety of colors here, how they change and intermingle. I think it even makes me afraid that everything I was ever taught, or perhaps more importantly, that I evolved (or so I believed), in my own thinking and beliefs, was so far off."

As these thoughts formed in and coursed through my mind, the questions were either answered or expanded with more theories in a manner only made capable by my newly granted intellectual abilities. Initially, I reacted to "Sources'" answer and my interpretation of what the shading of the lights might mean on a very "human" level. This revelation was being delivered to me through that mysterious osmosis type system that spoke and felt so kindly and softly to me that I was momentarily taken off guard. I said, thought, again, "Then why do I fear staying, returning, or fear anything at all? And is there a social order?"

So softly came the message that my building anxiety diminished, immediately allowing me to relax and truly hear and absorb the heightened perspective being presented to me. The many wonderful transfixing experiences of my "transition" caused me to momentarily forget, and I was gently reminded that I was in just that—in transition, and therefore, I was yet tethered to my earthly existence. Twin influences, so to speak. I had been so overwhelmed with the rush of everything that, well, it's not that I forgot what was happening "back home", really. I felt assured that I could return should I choose to and trusted completely in whomever and whatever I encountered in this place (although they told me it was a site of illusion). I was immersed in my new surroundings, until my human influences tugged at me.

"Fear is so deeply imbedded in the cellular human construct that it may take quite a while to unrecognize it. It is only a well-rehearsed reaction. Fear, as well as many diseases, often are treated here in settings similar to hospitals. Transitioning can be a traumatic experience for many, especially those that suffered long term."

My perception of this showed itself to me in soft forms; forms Source created so that my hybrid self could comprehend what I'll describe as translucent and pulsating light figures functioning in structures not unlike our hospital buildings. The equipment and method of care was strange, alien even; yet obviously kind and effective. The glimpse I was being given flickered a bit behind waves of energy, almost like seeing it through the heat rising off the desert floor, causing me to feel like an honored guest allowed private access to this information.

I became aware that there was a stillness in my mind, a quiet. As I observed the healers going about their duties, sounds, thoughts and communications from Source suddenly paused, switching my sense of being an honored guest to now feeling voyeuristic and oddly out of place. The abrupt silence completely upset what little was left of my equilibrium and without delay, took me directly to feeling constrained by... fear!

Still seeing the strange healing colony buzzing silently before me, Source remained silent while my thoughts returned. "What am I afraid of?" was the first thing to cross my mind. For as long as I can remember, I truly have believed that fear, in all of its manners and expressions, is man and woman-kind's Achilles' heel. I consciously have made the effort not to buy into it. Of course, I have my phobias and fears. I've worked hard to minimize them and have, in small ways, overcome some. Black Widow spiders, they still get to me! I have gotten better. I no longer destroy them on sight. If possible, I avoid them and let them be. I haven't ardently feared death; I have feared a painful or long, agonizing one, but who doesn't? Heights! I just haven't gotten through that one, yet. I admit it! Heights more than get my attention. Driving on a freeway overpass earns goosebumps; glass elevators I avoid or stand in the back, facing the rear.

Overall, I've been up and down and over and out (like the song says) so many times that I've come to believe in myself and the fact (in my case, anyway) that things tend to work out okay, in the end. In my life, in this current incarnation, as I matured, fear was a reaction or an emotion of which its harmful effects I was absolutely aware of and remained vigilant against. Or perhaps, maybe not so much. Perhaps I thought way too highly of myself and my advancements, spiritual or otherwise, and my quest against the cancer-causing agent known as fear. Maybe my new-found pal Source was not-so-gently trying to tell me something...

Douglas' form became more solid as he thought to me, distinguishing himself clearly from the other pulsating light forms.

"Let it go, Peter. It's only an illusion, a tool for teaching. Do you see how fear, kindness and love has directed your life? Remember, Peter. Think," I heard him whisper into my thoughts.

His form "touched" me and when he did, we merged at the contact point and I was immediately returned to earlier that day, where I sat on the edge of my bath shrouded in gratitude once again.

Cradled safely in the clasp of Source," I again was guided to observe my life-review. This time, however, the focus was on my relationship with fear, and how it was introduced and then integrated into my life. A scene from when I was three or four years old jumped into my mind. I was sitting outside at the top of the long steps to our home when a large black wasp landed on my chest. The stark contrast to my crisp white t-shirt only seemed to enhance its size, which against my four foot frame already looked huge. I was petrified. I recall screaming for Pinky, our nanny and housekeeper, all while being so still, afraid to move a muscle. I sat there, terrified, as the scariest creature I had ever encountered slowly crawled across my stomach, its wings vibrating and thorax twitching menacingly. In my recollection, I didn't breathe for minutes, not until dear sweet Pinky came to my rescue. Pinky understood immediately what was needed and took care of both the wasp and me. She quickly and gently removed the wasp, letting it fly free. Once it was gone, she scooped me up and sat down with me in her lap and explained to me that I had nothing to fear from that wasp. Yes, if it was scared, it may have stung me, but other than being aware of that, there was no reason to fear it. In a few simple actions, Pinky taught me a lesson that I have thought of often throughout my lifetime. Be aware of your surroundings and respectful of nature and others. Be kind, but not fearful.

Other pictures from my childhood flashed with the corresponding fear or insecurity, followed by an immediate immersion of communication with Source," resulting in my total understanding of the process. This proceeded throughout my entire life-review, repeating to explore and understand the effects of "kindness" and "love" as well as "fear."

Music from my bedroom stereo swelled in and around and through me and my universe; beautifully commanding my complete attention. It wasn't just any music, but a favorite song that I've loved since my teens, a song I'd performed hundreds of times, each time in tribute to this very version that now consumed my thoughts. Tried as I might, I couldn't think of anything other than remaining immersed in the magic that is Frank Sinatra and Antonio Carlos Jobim's performance of Jobim's classic "Dindi" (Gin-Gee). All I could do was muster a smile while basking in their artistic brilliance.

Once the song ended, I continued to sit with the warm, thick towel wrapped around me for a minute more. My feelings of being off balance were overcome with the excitement of the evening that awaited me. Still, when I rose, I rose with care and wondered what had weakened me. Taking that extra few minutes to rest and enjoy, listening to Sinatra and Jobim helped strengthen me. Kim had given me a beautiful scarf, so I chose my wardrobe for the evening to match it. Feeling a bit better and, if I say so myself, looking pretty good, too, I arrived at a local club where I had a weekly show with plenty of time to eat before we started. I hadn't eaten much that day and thought that had contributed to my feeling weak earlier, and still, I really didn't have an appetite. I ordered a bowl of soup and enjoyed their famous bread with a cup of coffee, and I felt ready to go… I called my guitar player over and had him add the song "Dindi" to the set, just for shits and giggles. The club filled up with familiar faces. People stopped by my table and chatted for a moment, some old pals and some new. I was beginning to feel good.

The band did their opening numbers and then brought me up, and as usual, it seemed like the show was over in a flash. It was great fun! The regulars mixed with the newcomers, making a warm, receptive and wonderful crowd. Tonight, my friends and bandmates were fantastic! I did struggle some, I'll admit. That nagging unsteadiness… the weakness. I'm not sure, really, how else to describe it. I had hoped the soup would help, and it did a bit… I got through it. We had a good show, a fun night and I started saying my good nights and thank yous right away, so I could be home by nine p.m. You know you're gettin' high in hours when you're happy to be home by nine p.m.! Well, tonight, seeing as I was dragging a little, I was all too happy to get back to the castle early.

I drove up the driveway just in time to catch our grandson and three of Kim's boys as they reached the bottom of the stairs. Once I parked, Matty ran over and opened my car door for me, explaining as he did that, they were going for ice cream and then to the beach and then to Von's for something or other, I don't know what, and he did this all-in-one breath! WHEW! Impressive! He's got some lungs for a little guy! Maybe he should be a horn player instead of a drummer! He was so cute and excited. Kids, they are so pure with their emotions. He was beaming and was so happy that I got home so he could tell me about his upcoming adventure. I got a quick hug and a promise for more later before Matty ran off with his uncles and I climbed the stairs to our house.

"You just missed the kids," Kim said as I entered the kitchen.

"No, I saw them in the driveway. Matty was so cute. He was so excited to tell me they were going for ice cream and the beach, and he just kept going on and on… I was afraid he'd pass out if he didn't take a breath!" I laughed. Kim finished what she was doing and crossed to where I stood. While giving me a welcome home hug, she whispered in my ear those words I loved to hear, "We're alone in the house, dear..."

For the first time in my life, I can say I have someone who, no matter what is happening, brings reason and positivity to me. My days, as corny as it may sound, are brightened each time I see her. I absolutely love her face... it truly makes me happy! Yes, I am in love. As I laid there, trying not to drift off to sleep, I was conscious of the smile I had because of the woman next to me, and for the world she opened up for me; I reflected on the near perfect day that I'd just enjoyed, still fighting the heaviness of sleep that was creeping in. Then, nothing. And then that shocking pain.

Minute Four

My decision to remain here with Douglas and my other pals or return to my family was causing me more anguish than imaginable. Suddenly, I seemed to feel the polarity of everything. My ever-growing bond with Source was unexpectedly contrasted by my distrust of my having been given the choice of staying or returning. Rather than seeing this as the gift I first thought it was, I now, without warning, was distrustful. *This can't be Heaven,* I thought.

"I already told you it's not, Pedro. Like Bobby said, this place has room for illusions. It's an area where we can explore and understand our transitions, teach, learn, even visit to guide our loved ones. It is also a place to expand from one reality form and unify it with your spirit form and ultimately, with Source," Douglas said to refocus me. He understood that I was totally confused. I was questioning just about everything! Why did I have this choice? I had too many things to say and so little time...

"Let it go, brother. Where would you be most comfortable? Go big, anywhere at all," he asked me.

"Bali. I've always wanted to go there," I said to my old pal. And instantly, we were there! The lavish scenery was more stunning in person than pictures had ever displayed. The ocean was a color of blue and green that I'd never seen or even imagined. Beautiful birds and flowers spotted brightness into the emerald green of the dense forest. Everywhere I looked I was surrounded by natural wonders so exquisite that surely, they had to rival those in Heaven. If this wasn't in fact Heaven; it sure looked like it to me.

"Thanks, Douglas! That was quick! That's why I never went to Bali. I hated long plane flights. Just look at this, man! It would have been worth it, the long flight. Look at what I missed!"

"About that, Peter, my man. Why didn't you like flying?"

"I flew a lot as a young man, and traveled over most of the world, but as I got older, Douglas, I wasn't so comfortable being 30,000 feet in the air! I developed a mild phobia, I guess. I flew only when necessary."

"Fear got ya!" Douglas teased.

And he was right. Simple and to the point. A perfect example of how fear affected my life. We wandered down a crescent shaped beach on a calm lagoon which led us to a pair of lounge chairs that overlooked an outcropping of mango trees.

We stood for a moment, quietly enjoying what must be getting near to the final time we could enjoy each other's company before my decision affected these matters; or was I limiting my scope of vision by being yet tied to my physical being?

While standing shoulder to elbow (his six foot five to my five foot seven), Douglas broke into laughter, saying, "You are one lucky hombre! No wonder you're having a hard time makin' up your mind! Your final day was damn near perfect." He leaned down to tease me. "One of your major fears was avoided! How lucky can one guy get?"

Waving his hand to prevent me from interrupting, he excitedly continued with his theory of my confusion and hesitation. In answer to the question that he knew was forming in my mind, he reminded me how I feared a long, lingering and painful death.

"You had two sharp pains, and wait, no! You had two QUICK sharp pains, and BANG! You were free floating up around your bedroom ceiling wondering if you were having a bad dream until I came along to straighten things out. And it's not the first time I've bailed you out, either, come to think of it!"

"God, you're right. That's a pretty simple way of looking at it, Douglas. I've always been lucky, even in the toughest times. And if that does turn out to be my last day, it was a great one. And my getting out with two quick painful jolts, well, with all the horrible countless other options, that was like winning the lottery. Especially with my background! And, yes, dear friend. You did save my life that fateful Valentine's Day. Come on! I already told that story and said nice things about you in my first book!"

"And why did you say nice things, because I'm a nice guy? Or was!" Douglas happily chimed in.

With a smile still implanted on his face, he explained that no matter how simple, that was only half of the equation. So much more awaited me in this realm. I had only been privy to a glimpse beyond the welcoming plane where Douglas and Bobby had greeted me. I had yet to fully understand or appreciate what it was to be one with Source, having just scratched the surface, so to speak. And perhaps we would explore them now, certainly soon. One common element to be dealt with, regardless of my decision, was fear.

"When you died a couple of minutes ago, you died a loved man. You died without prolonged pain or suffering after having lived one of the most full and interesting lives of anyone I've ever known. Those are on the side of staying. Whether you stay or go, this is an opportunity to expand your spirituality. To do so takes truly facing your fear. Do it here, and we will guide you. Return before confronting this, and you're on your own," Douglas only half teased.

Fear. What a contrary concept to the magnificent beauty that surrounded us.

Upon sitting, I was transported to a time of my youth. As a toddler I was sensing the fear of separation. My father was a seaman and would go to sea for three or four months at a time. I got used to this quickly. This, as I recall, wasn't a big deal. What I remembered was late at night, lying in bed while my sister and mother were sleeping, wondering what would become of me if something happened to my mother. I feared being separated from her. My youthful dread wasn't my father leaving; he was always leaving. When he was home, it never felt that he was there, really. He kept busy with business projects and television acting pursuits, not fatherly ones. He was never unkind or mean. He just wasn't too interested in me. He was crazy about my sister, and oddly, I was okay with that. I must have been blessed from birth with great survival skills and picked up on this as a baby, because I don't recall a time when I relied on him. For anything. Therefore, the thought of my mother dying and me being left without her became my main boogeyman as a toddler. My first fear.

The memories came rushing at me in forms I'll describe as being similar to photos flashing erratically throughout my field of vision, each photo generating another; each with its own analysis of my fear's beginnings as well as their effects on my life. First came the fears of a child; then those of a boy; then of a teen; then a young man's, a husband, a father's, a grandfather. Prejudice, bigotry, any and all forms of ignorance and hate that I had bought into throughout my life washed through like sewage.

It was ugly. Seeing what was programmed into me by "well-intentioned" folks, parents, general family, teachers, preachers, media, etc. blew my everlovin' mind! Admitting to buying into as much as I did, well... I didn't, for a long time.

As with many of us, my views changed as I aged. I once heard it put this way: "Your sharp edges get rounded in time." It makes sense to me. Maturing must bring some wisdom and clarity, letting you see the cracks in the arguments of those things you feared or hated or misunderstood. It even let me see the cracks in my arguments and where I'd been wrong. Ouch!

Aging taught me that many of the fixations that I initially misunderstood or was just plain wrong about were not worth pursuing, such as racial prejudice and its multitude of corresponding fears. Time softened many of my more rigid, youthful opinions, leaving me with fewer fear-based issues as a sixty-seven-year-old guy than when I was a younger man. Boyhood fears melt away and morph into more age-appropriate shadows and demons. Demons that as an adult seem so real, that if given in to, may result in real life consequences. Even spiritual consequences.

I did not need my heightened awareness and intellect to recognize this in my life review. Of late, I had been happily aware of my patterns of avoidance and denial I developed over the years. Hell, it doesn't take a shrink to figure mixed up little 'ol me out! I was able, however, with the aid of my expanded abilities, to immediately go deeply into the initiation of my fears and sense of inadequacy, and then see the growth out of and away from such thoughts or beliefs (or not).

And fear still raises its evil little head! I'm no Zen Master, let's remember! And then a fear arose in my head that I could not stop. I wished I could separate myself from Source and Douglas and any one or thing that was listening or connected to my thoughts because all I could think of was how happy I was that I got away with such a short review of my "negative" consequences. My connection to my human side apparently held residual guilt and shame. My inability to hide this thought exposed my vulnerability and embarrassment to Source, and to my old and dear friend, Douglas. It's like I ratted on myself. I couldn't stop!

Momentarily feeling exposed in a manner that bared my body, mind, and spirit, with a bright flash not unlike being photographed, my current lifetime's hurtful effects on others were frozen in thought and pictures. The pictures shifted, flew and flashed before me, much like those had when reviewing my fears.

Flashes of disappointed friends and lovers. Scenes of unrealized dreams and deals and how others were left in their wake...

There was no judgement here. Not from Source. Definitely not from Douglas. The only sense of judgement was mine. Assessment is key to self-growth and contribution to Source. To judge, versus assess, brings with it a whole different set of notions... like good old Catholic (and Jewish) guilt! And eleven years of Catholic school, no matter how little of the theology I signed up for, exposed me to an unhealthy heaping of it, which sadly rubbed off!

"So, here's the 'Hellfire' part, huh? I'm going to relive all of my sins and feel the pain I inflicted on everyone, right?" I mumbled more to myself than to any one or thing as I remained caught up in the swirl of my life from this awful vantage point. I was sharing the pain I now saw that I had caused, and each injustice, large or small, came and went, bringing with it pain and leaving behind understanding. And, like everything that I'd encountered here so far, it was over in what seemed to be just a moment. The impression left was indominable, however. The pain, deep and profound. The self-contrition, also intense and reflective.

"Is this the way it works for everybody, or is this unique to me? Is this just what I expected it to be? Hmmmm?" I silently wondered.

"It's pretty much what you want it to be. It always has been, Peter. Always."

The voice in my head saying this was familiar; too familiar for me not to know it, yet I couldn't quite place it. I looked to Douglas for clarity, who offered none. He simply gave a knowing grin and motioned with his head that I should look to my left, where the fine sand gave way to the thick jungle under-bush

Looking left, the foliage was lush. Dark green faded to lighter shades of green, yellow and orange. Bright flowers dotted the landscape adding blues, purples and reds; and in contrast to the smooth beige sand at its feet and the deep blue sky overhead, this dense blanket of color was magnificent! Every aspect of what I expected Bali to be burst forth at that moment. Birds of unbelievable plumage flew and squawked! Jungle sounds swelled, as did the scents of the lagoon. The sun gently warmed us as we sat taking in the astounding beauty that was my vision of Bali. Who knew if any of this was even close to the real Bali, but who cares? I was happy.

Then a fog playfully rose from the ground where the jungle began, rising to the height of the lower palm trees. It, too, was exceptionally beautiful. Weird, but stunning in that it was backlit and seemed to be changing hues, very subtly, all in the shades of white to pink. A sheen danced off its surface like moonlight bouncing off sea swells, making the curtain of mist even more mystical. If a breeze was stirring, it would have stopped. If the sound of birds singing filled the air, this powerful presence, I'm sure, would have quieted their songs. As far as I knew, everything had stopped. I was completely focused on this semi-theatrical scene being presented for me. It was all encompassing. The air around Douglas and me grew heavy with anticipation as this eerie layer of fog thickened and danced.

And for the first time since my arrival here, wherever this transition place was, I heard music. As an opening in the fog slowly started, almost teasingly so, a drumbeat could be softly heard. A flute soon joined in and when a man emerged through the fog, followed by what looked like a crowd of men, women and kids, all I could hear was a pounding in my head with them all saying in unison… "I am you; you are us; we are one." Although they each spoke their native tongue, I understood them simultaneously as naturally as I now do English. This chant got louder as more people were revealed and the fog lifted, finally displaying along the curved bay what looked to be hundreds of people. They were dressed in the garb of their time, in styles that ranged from the last century to ancient times.

"Douglas?" I asked sheepishly, while not taking my eyes off the huge mob.

"Yeah, well, this is wild even for this place, pal! I'm not sure. I think it is only a reflection of your expectations. You always had an innovative mind, so enjoy your movie! I am! And I can't wait to see what all these people are here for!" Douglas replied.

"You mean you don't know? What kind of guide are you, for cryin' out loud?" I said while starting to sense something familiar about a man that had stepped out from the crowd. He walked up to me and before he could say a word, I knew who he was. As impossible as it may seem, any place other than this place, I knew that what he was now saying was only confirming what I knew in my soul to be true. He was me, in my most recent incarnation. They all were me. And I, them. All 826 of them, us… I mean, me!

I felt as if I were a vessel. I stood before my prior selves and opened my arms to them, and was drained of all contents: thoughts, knowledge, wisdom, beliefs, and dreams. As each of them came into my embrace, they melded into my being and consciousness, and in that instant, showed me that lifetime in its entirety, all the while adding to the pool of knowledge and wisdom, filling that vessel with everything that was now me.

Once again, although this process repeated itself 826 times, it all happened in the blink of an eye.

"Far fuckin' out!" Douglas burst out laughing. "That was one of the most mind- blowin' things I've seen yet, Peter, my man! You have got some kind of imagination! I should have written more scripts with you, man! You are flipping me out, brother! I'm lovin' your vision, man! Keep goin'… this is great! Great!"

"This is the best you've seen! How long have you been here, now? Four, five years? I've been here a few minutes and I'm settin' records already? Whaddya do all the time around here, Douglas? You're supposed to help me out here! Well, I'm glad that I'm at least entertaining you!" I sarcastically spit out.

Yet what had just happened freaked me out, too. 826 previous lifetimes. *Is that a lot?* I wondered. We are talking about all of eternity, here, after all. Well, the past part, anyway. And so many female lifetimes... 568 to be exact. Each person was so unique, yet they carried a trait that showed a familiar relationship to each other. Instantly upon coming into my embrace, they were not simply recognized; they and their (my) entire life's history was known, absorbed in that strange yet effective process much like osmosis that I'd been blessed with since coming into this astonishing and expansive realm. Languages did not present barriers, and the different time periods spanning hundreds of years back to my last incarnation represented were truly bewildering.

"So, it's true! You really are an old soul!" Douglas choked as he laughed at his own purposely lame joke.

"Compared to what, my friend? I saw you in a lot of my lifetimes... My mind was too freaked out by the whole thing to think about it then, but now that I do think about it, we've been hanging out together for a long time. Did you notice that, too?"

"Yeah, sure, I noticed. I also know that we've been travelling in the same circles, so to speak, for hundreds of lifetimes. Weird, huh? You asked earlier if there is a caste system here, for lack of a better term. The simple answer is, yes. It is primarily based on experience and the collection and expression of wisdom. To acquire these takes time... many lifetimes of experience as a child, woman, man, and all of the variations of life and death experiences imaginable. You ask, is 826 lifetimes a lot? The word on the street, my friend, is that it depends on what you do with them! Capice, paisano?"

"In your case, I think that's a question for you and Source to work through together. The general idea, I think, is to gather up some defenses against fear and ignorance, and to not let fear drive you beyond basic survival instinct. When fear is a driving factor, it is self-defeating. Understand that pain, physical, emotional and or spiritual pain, is at the root of fear, with death and its litany of related maladies being the ultimate trepidation. With each lifetime, like a maturing human during its life, knowledge and experiences change its perspective. Fear, which was originally meant as a protective device, just for flight or fight, grew so out of hand and is so deeply ingrained in humanity, that it can take some time and rehabilitation on this plane to correct it spiritually. Does that sound more like I'm helping you out, puttin' your mind at ease, old buddy? Huh? Do I have to be serious all the time to be believable, now?" he chided.

"Be as snide as you like, Dougy! But please, let's not forget that I'm dyin' here!" That old show-biz reference to having a bad show once again brought a smile to both of our faces, even though the current reference held far greater consequences. Greater consequences, yet certainly not graver ones.

I now realized that there was nothing to fear. That does not mean that I stopped feeling that churning that sits deep in your intestines. No, only that now I understood what Douglas meant regarding fear's proper function. Still having one foot on earth, so to speak, my understanding of this did not stop me from having a reaction—a typical human one, at that. I was also starting to see that recovering from the scars left by deeply ingrained fears would require serious spiritual healing.

"You don't look like you're dyin'..." Douglas leaned in close to say, and before he could complete his thought, I did it for him.

"Because I'm not! How can I die when I just relived my previous 826 lifetimes? We both watched as they came into me; each life strung to the next, yet totally different. There is a continuity that defies the concept of death. It is more like a constant round of renewal that includes this stop. From the earth plane, we can't see this place, so we've been taught that it's a place to fear. Now that I'm straddling both planes, I can see that pretty clearly. There is no death or dying!"

"Listen to you! Just a few minutes poking only half of your fine old self around 'up here' and you think you've got it all figured out! Well, I guess I'm not surprised after what I just witnessed... 826 'youz' going into YOU! How could you NOT be full of yourself?" Douglas snickered.

"You couldn't resist, could ya? Maybe it's a sad comment about me, but I've missed your 'jokes', pal," I said as I smiled at my old and truly brilliant friend, although you may not know it from his latest attempt at humor.

"Control! How easy is that!" I thought, referring to fear, of course. If the basic design of fear was to protect us from danger, then turning it around and using fear to control people jumped into my mind as such an easy thing to do. And, again, from my temporarily expanded mental abilities, it appeared to be elemental. In human terms, it only took a really smart, devious and socially experienced person. Or perhaps a religious one, depending on your point of view. My mind was spinning with concepts mixed with real life experiences and recalled memories when suddenly I heard dogs barking. Their excited barking came from the same direction that all 826 of my former selves had come, and they were bounding our way!

"More former self revelations, my friend?" Douglas laughed as he kneeled down to greet the first barking, tail-wagging arrival, who ignored him and jumped into my surprised arms.

"Snickers!" I nearly yelled once I recognized her. As little Snickers covered me in kisses and squiggled in my arms, I was just able to see that the other dogs, cats and birds coming on this chaotic scene were my former pets!

"You bet, Douglas! They reveal the best part of me! Are you sure this isn't Heaven?" I asked as I sat on the edge of the lounge chair and hugged and kissed as many of my lovely pets as I could. Wherever this was, right now, it was my heaven!

On that hypnotic beach in Bali, surrounded by my loving pets from my most recent lifetime, with the thoughts of 826, perhaps 827, lifetimes being shared with my dear friend Douglas, I had a clarifying vision. For one moment, it seemed as if I could merge with the truth of what Source was exposing me to. I could feel it. I was it. The pure, uncomplicated love of my pets for me and me for them was a simple catalyst to that truth. A pathway away from fear that enabled me to connect to Source without inhibition or hesitation. Without humanity or ego. It was freeing and elegant. It also contributed to my state of confusion regarding the minutes old question, "should I stay, or should I go?"

I wanted to stay for the experience of all that awaited me. I realized that I had only seen the tip of the iceberg, and what lay ahead was so tempting. I have always been a curios cat, and since I was already dead (mostly, anyway), I didn't have to worry about curiosity being my undoing.

I also wanted to return. The thought of not being with Kim and our grandson was not sitting well with me. If I returned, I could be there for them, in whatever way, yet now that seemed to be in teaching. Teaching that fear, in all of its forms, needs to be recognized, faced and dealt with, stripped and seen for what it so often is: evil manipulation. My furious funnel of thoughts, just prior to my old pets coming on the scene, were showing me that if this turned out to be a "near death experience", it would load me up with a whole lot of information to share.

I was sensing that I now had an innate understanding of the inner workings of Source and was somehow given a special dispensation in order to have such a unique choice of staying or going. I was overcome with a sense of buoyancy at the thought that I perhaps was being given a second chance to get things right by returning with this knowledge, should I choose to do so. Suddenly, as I was about to announce my decision to Douglas and Source, through the crowd of excited, semi-jealous pets, jumped two of my all-time favorite dogs, vying as always for my attention: Pilot and Charlie. They were hurdling themselves at me, growling and mock-fighting each other as I pet them while looking in shock at Douglas, and then at the nearly stopped, super-slow-motion scene still in my bedroom, where Pilot and Charlie were on the floor, huddled together, visibly shaken by the tension in the room.

"What the f..." I was cut off by Charlie's sloppy, wet kiss, right on my mouth!

As my wonderful animals wandered around the small bay, Pilot, Charlie and Snickers, who did die two years ago, rubbed and pushed up against me as we hadn't seen each other in years. As their excitement continued, so did my curiosity.

"Douglas, these dogs are still alive! What's goin' on, man? What are they doin' here? Oh, my GOD!" I gasped. "Did something happen to them? To all of them?"

"No, no, everyone's fine, Peter."

"Then how did my dogs... why are my... Wait, Douglas," I stammered, and as I did, I saw from a distance, peeking out from the jungle underbrush, my playful, puckish grandson. Followed by his momma, my beautiful Kim. As they stood there looking our way, it crossed my mind that it was only a moment ago that I thought that I knew what was going on around here. Now, I didn't have a clue.

"Yup, you were feelin' pretty full of yourself again, Paisan!" I said to myself, this time. And for a minute there, I was. Since seeing Kim, Matty, Pilot and Charlie, I was feeling a bit more deflated.

"Yet you're catchin' on, aren't you?" Douglas shouted over the barking and bird squawking.

"Smile don't frown! Think up, not down! Jump up and turn around! Take your thinking way uptown!" He see-song sang and danced like a crazy man, with cats, dogs and birds all delighting in his energy!

"What the hell are you talking about, Douglas? Catching on to what? Since we've been on this beach, so much has gone down I don't know what to make of it except that..."

Then, my rant was interrupted from the essence of Source, who simultaneously provided comfort and answers, again by that strange osmosis like process. It took but a split-second, so fast that I continued my thought.

"...we exist on all planes, at all times. How else could Kim and Matty be standing over there? And the dogs be here? That's what makes sense to me. Wait! There's more. There's more, Douglas..."

The message Source imparted settled into me as my voice trailed off momentarily.

"...so much more to this, old friend!" Then, like a lightbulb went off, a revelation flashed, and I excitedly said, "Do you see this? You must! Douglas, tell me, what's the catch? Please, man. If I can really access both realms from here, tell me, why would I want to leave? Why, if time in fact does not exist, would I not simply 'wait' here, if waiting is even a thing anymore, for everyone and everything that I love to join me here? For that matter, what is any of this about, man? If Source knows it all already, and I am 'Source,' and all time is already known, and is already experienced, then what's it all about? What's it for? Is it just a circular game that endlessly rotates and recycles our bodies and souls, making slight adjustments and scenarios with each new round?"

"Are you done?" a semi-amused Douglas tried to interject.

"What are you smirking at, Douglas? This whole dying thing wasn't supposed to be so weird, man! Every time I feel like I'm starting to understand what's going on around here, someone or something pulls the carpet out from under me! I'm beginning to envy those peeps that have a clear vision of Heaven and Hell. Plain as day. Bam! They die, go up or down, or wait it out and cook for a while in the middle, and then it's over. Clear as a bell. Yet for me, I am getting exactly what I expected. And I am very confused. And guess what, old pal? You are not helping!"

His continued smirky grin normally would have really annoyed me, yet my being so wrapped up in my confusion put that on the back burner... for now. It's not that I didn't notice, it's just that I was coming to grips with the thought that maybe the musical genius Frank Zappa was right when he said, referring to all things religious and metaphysical, "Who you tryin' to jive with that cosmic debris?"

My mind once again was starting to spin out of control, having thoughts and memories that I was attempting to direct towards a conclusion, only to find more confusion. The more I reviewed all that had been shown to me, the more baffled I became. What purpose could so many lifetimes have individually, and to what purpose do they lead to collectively, if any, Mr. Zappa? I silently asked myself along with the maestro.

To understand the level of my disorientation, simply recall that I just quoted and sought advice from Frank Zappa!

And why not? Zappa may not be the first "Frank" you may associate me with, seeing as my tastes and talents go more in the direction of Frank Sinatra than Frank Zappa, although in my youth, I often sat around getting stoned with my musician pals marveling at Zappa's musical genius while laughing hysterically at his outrageous lyrics. And here I go again... spinning off on another tangent...another crazy direction of thought that leads to nothing of importance...

"Hey! Stop being so stuck! Never mind... it takes being here a while, pardon me, I forgot, there, old pal!" Douglas thankfully interrupted my self-imposed mind tornado again.

"Whaddaya mean, it takes a while? What takes a while?"

"Being less human. It is so powerful to inhabit a body and with a joined spirit, experience a lifetime of extreme encounters. To be able to view matters from a position free of ego and judgement requires experience seeing matters only from your spirit side, your place here with 'Source.' I'm trying very hard not to say that it's gonna take some time to get used to things around here…"

I jumped in and cut him off, somewhat annoyed, "Don't start sugarcoating shit now, Douglas! Trying hard not to say… what?"

"That it takes time, Peter, because time is such an illusion here. Like your seeing Kim and your grandson—another illusion, of sorts. Yet let's not go off on another wild goose chase! These are not important questions to ask now…"

"They seem important to me, pal! Kim and Matty were way off in the distance, so I don't know, but Pilot and Charlie, my dogs that are right now alive and well, THEY ARE NO ILLUSION! They are in both places at once, man, and right now, I gotta know what's goin' on!"

"Slow down your mind, Peter. E-a-s-y, now, this is not too difficult," he slowly and overly exaggerated in a semi-whisper, while gesturing broadly overhead with his arms in a protracted semi-circle.

"Don't mock me, Douglas! I'm locked in a train of thought that..."

And then it hit me. He wasn't mocking me. He was right. My wild, hippie-dancing friend had once again distracted me so that I could cross the gap from human perception to whatever this was... and as my thoughts slowed to a pace that I could decipher them, it was clear the difference between man and animal, and the purity of their souls. Animals were allowed to breach the Veil between planes and freely visit at will. Humans, not so much. Not really. Just for perhaps a short visit. Like the one I was having.

"The veil! If I go back, will I remember any of this, Douglas?"

The thought of my dogs hanging out with me in both planes simultaneously reminded me of the concept of the Veil that separates the physical and spiritual worlds. My somewhat limited understanding of it basically puts it as a divide that keeps secret the mysteries of the heavens. Hence my question to good old Douglas, and, therefore, my latest dilemma.

"Some, maybe. Sure, you're gonna remember a bit, something, I think..." he nonchalantly, almost bored, really, responded.

"I'm not too sure, really, come to think of it. People remember the bright light…maybe that's what you'll remem…"

I abruptly cut him off, "What the hell are you doing? I'm not playing, Douglas! If I go back, can I teach them that all fear is bullshit? Will I have the right words, the right way to say and show those people around me the truth, or will all that I'm being made privy to here be lost… unless I stay? Or is the Veil', the very thing put in place to maintain Sources' domain over humanity, the very device to create questions regarding eternity and surround the unknown in mystery, the genesis of fear?"

Hearing my own words chilled me. Imagine if fear was born of Sources' or God's intention, and assuming that the God or Source is not an all-knowing being as I was fed at Catholic school as a kid, but an ever-evolving essence, one that maybe had programmed a fatal human flaw.

Along with my suspicion that Source may not be all-knowing, it suddenly occurred to me that the implied perfection of Source or God (also heavily programmed in my youth) was also flawed, giving way to an even more cynical and dark set of possibilities.

"You've been here, for what, a few minutes? And you're ready to start a fight already!" Douglas teased, as he obviously enjoyed my continuing confusion.

"Before you spin yourself into oblivion, allow me to remind you," he said with a British accent and air of autocracy, "that you still have one foot in Heaven, so to speak, and one still on earth..."

"Meaning?" I interjected.

"Meaning," he continued to drone, "that you don't yet have a clue, darling!" And with that declaration, Douglas tossed his head and snapped his fingers, as if to dismiss his loyal subjects, here being played by the gaggle of my previous pets; he was still quite enjoying himself. He's always been a bit odd, this old friend of mine. I suppose it is part of his charm.

The realization that the root belief that God, or Source is all-good and all-knowing had been churning unnoticed deeply imbedded within in my sub-conscience surprised me. I had been exposed to the teachings of the Catholic church from my time as a toddler through the tenth grade, when I was sixteen, when I left an all-boys Catholic high school for public education. Yet by then I had been heavily programmed to their way of thinking, although I thought that I had rid myself of much of their doctrine. And now, here I was, wrestling with an existential question of tremendous proportions: could the God- Source be the creator of fear and all of fear's cancerous consequences?

"Stop!" I yelled at myself to stop thinking this way.

"What's wrong with me, Douglas?"

"I was just gonna ask you the same thing."

I cut him off... "Thanks, smart ass! Really, man, have I lost it, or what? I've got the whole world…more than that! I've got more than the whole universe, Douglas, to check out, to visit, and what am I doin'? I'm spinnin' out of control on things like the origination of fear. I gotta just stop! Right now! And please, pal, help keep me on track, would ya? God knows I need some guidance, here."

And as I said this, I recalled an old expression, and feeling if it was appropriate, I silently brought it to mind. "Jesus H. Christ!"

Minute Five

"Whadaya think the 'H' stands for, guys?" an unfamiliar voice from behind me gleefully asked.

Before turning to see our new guest, I looked up and noticed that Douglas, who was facing both of us, had a delighted and somewhat amused expression on his face. I saw him wink at me as a smile spread across his face. I spun to greet what I presumed would be another favorite "someone" from my past, as I felt I may be on my own personal "This Is Your Life" review, once again. Yet, the man I encountered upon completing my turn, while hearing Douglas from behind me respond to the afore-mentioned question,

"Horatio?", was not from my past. Not really. He was dressed quite nattily in a loose-fitting cotton outfit suitable for the beach and was deeply tanned, not dressed as I usually thought of him; but I knew him immediately.

"Horatio!" Christ laughed loudly in response to Douglas' guess. Sensing my skepticism, our new visitor looked me squarely in my eyes, and with a smile more captivating than I've ever seen, without words or physical contact, convinced me that he was no mere illusion. He was the guy. The real deal. Jesus H. Christ.

Having been caught completely off guard, and without forethought, the true smart-ass in me arrived...

"So, what is it?" I asked. I don't see you as a 'Horatio'! 'Harmony', maybe! 'Jesus Harmony Christ'! I like that! I think that makes more sense, with you bringing peace and harmony to the world and all, and, oh, wait... ehhh, ah, well, hey, ya did your best! No, that's too corny. Maybe you're more of a regular guy type..." I rattled on, more out of an onset of nerves than anything, when, thank God, he cut me off.

"It's just 'H', as far as I know. That seems to be what most folks say, anyway. Honestly, I've not given it too much thought. Yet I do like 'Horatio', Douglas!" Christ said as he walked to where Douglas stood, then embraced him. Turning to me with an arm around Christ's waist, Douglas, with a look of contentment and pride, formally introduced me to his eminent comrade.

"Peter, meet who was my guide, Jesus. With or without the 'H'." Douglas winked at us as he said this. Both Jesus and I winced and chuckled at Douglas' lame joke. I was starting to like this Jesus guy. "When you transitioned, you got me and all my wisdom waiting for you, hanging around a beautiful beach, while I got Him waiting for me at an altar of worship."

"I long ago came to believe that we find what we expect to when we transition," I responded, trying to be cool. Yet truth be known, standing here, talking to Jesus H. Christ, no less, was a pretty big deal... bigger even than meeting Frank Sinatra for the first time! And believe me... that was a big deal! Although I shed most of the teachings of Christianity, I always thought of Christ as an advanced spirit. One of a few truly powerful spiritual teachers that had walked the walk and talked the talk, before their message became convoluted and bastardized for other purposes. And as jaded as I had been at times in my life, I'd always held this Jesus fellow in high regard; among the highest, really. And here I was. Unexpectedly hanging out with the Man Himself! I have to admit, I was starstruck. Having nearly grown up in show business, my saying that is something! Then, more out of self-defense than anything else, again without forethought, I said to Douglas, "yet I figured your idea of Heaven would involve rock stars, concerts and after-parties."

"There was a time, that's for sure! We partied pretty hard back in the day!" Douglas laughed. "After my dad died, I started going to church again. I rediscovered the original Rock Star! It was only three years later until I transitioned and when I did, I got my vision of the afterlife. And my vision included Him."

As Douglas was speaking, an illusion formed around Christ. It was subtle, as if faint shards of light flickered off his shoulders, peeling off soundlessly and seemingly at the speed of light. They came at an alarming rate and would vanish as quickly as they appeared, all while going unnoticed or ignored by Christ. Noticing my having been distracted by his personal light show, Christ off-handedly explained,

"I'm big around here! Not that any of us are keeping score, but between me, Buddha, Allah, Brahman, and the more generic God, I'm holding down the number one position. What you're seeing is other peoples' images of Me that are needed elsewhere. Ya know what I mean?" Christ gave me a wry smile as I nodded my understanding.

Yet my mind drifted a bit as I tried to see more clearly just what Christ meant when he said, "other people's images of Me." Knowing this, He instantly made visible the shards of light as they left his shoulders. Versions of Jesus were as varied as one can imagine, yet they all seemed to have one trait in common: Jesus always had His arms open to welcome His children home.

This welcoming image brought to mind the thought that the very opposite vision had been missing. Nothing in my experience so far or the glimpses I'd been afforded had even hinted of anything dark or evil. The concept of punishment or Hell thus far hadn't raised its ugly little head...

"That's because Hell is a construct of the human mind, my friend. When one first transitions, no matter the beliefs of the individual, we protect them from that level of fear. No one faces fire and brimstone or eternal damnation when initially confronting the changes of transition. No. It is always a loving and warming experience, though it can be confusing. That is why no one dies, or more accurately, transitions, alone. Everyone is met at their time by the spirit of someone, or many, that they know, or even imagine, who gives them comfort and trust, so that they may move easily from one world to the next. Although we do this time and time again as we reincarnate, we forget, by design, and therefore, need reassurance and guidance. Regardless of your background and beliefs, or how you have lived your life, your spirit is welcomed upon its return. And as you are seeing, the importance of your soul and being to the Source is valued on an entirely different scale than the set of rules that exists on Earth that man has claimed and said that God designed. God did not design anything that punishes elements of itself. We are all part of the Source; the 'God-Source,' and as such, wouldn't it be incongruous and self-defeating to do so? Pretty silly when you think it through. Yet instilling fear, using the great unknown and grand concepts like God and eternity, and burning forever in Hell if you're not a good boy or girl, well, that was not too difficult to establish by intelligent leaders anxious to control the less rational masses."

"Interesting, Douglas," Christ chimed in.

"Whaddya mean, 'interesting, Douglas'?" I flippantly responded. "Isn't that right? It fits with what I've believed most of my life!" I replied to both of them.

The coolest dude in the world did what I would never have expected the coolest dude in the world (and beyond) to do—He scrunched His divine shoulders and, with palms upheld, simply shrugged, leaving it up to my judgment.

"No, no, no!" I said to Christ. "I'm not letting you off that easily! How 'bout you jump in here with your opinion. It seems to me that you, more than anyone in the entire universe, can shed a little light on the subject! So, what gives? Is Douglas right about these things... no Hell or eternal punishment? Come on, it's just us guys," I teased, knowing full well that He wasn't about to commit to anything. Yet I wanted to get to the heart of the matter with the one guy who could clear up all the mysteries. "Can I get a witness!?" I playfully sang out to Douglas, who's outstretched hand told me he had no desire to continue this conversation.

"C'mon! Douglas! Help me out here! You two seem to be pals. Talk to Him! It's all just a dream, all this, what's goin' on, really, isn't it… really? C'mon! Where's the harm in my knowing the truth? If I stay, I'll know anyway, won't I? And if I don't? The Veil will probably make me forget all this stuff. Which brings me to my next question…"

Christ reached over and touched my hand. My semi-agitated frame of mind, again at risk of spinning out of control, was calmed by this simple act. Wordlessly, even thoughtlessly, if you will imagine, we were informed that, in response to my un-asked questions, the laws of the universe and those of man often have little to do with one another. Well, that was the crux of the answer, anyway. Childhood cancer; world-wars; famine; and all forms of man's inhumanity towards man… those were not the queries I had in mind. Generally, I felt that I knew the reasons man needed those challenges. Man's desire to hunt and gather, search for truth and answers, will always require foils. Disease and monsters in human form will continually provide the motivation needed to propel those more forward-thinking souls towards solutions and society's advancements.

No, my confusions lay more with why one would choose life in human form, over and over, again in lieu of remaining in 'Heaven', or wherever or whatever 'this' really is? And what other forms of existence are there available to us; we are talking about eternity, after all? What does "This Plane" look like, if I let go and really see and experience it?

My mind, though now calm, was rapidly firing these thoughts. This refreshing clarity brought with it visions that I surmised were answers to my questions. Quick, still photo type answers that led to more questions... or perhaps these were mere distractions designed to derail me from probing further.

What purpose would be served by keeping me from knowing the back story to deep, dark—no, scratch that—to the deep, LIGHT and ever-expanding secrets of the universe? No purpose would be served. I answered my own question.

Before Douglas could, I playfully put the thought forward, "You're getting pretty full of yourself again, aren't you, Peter? Thinking that the secrets of the universe would be laid out for you, just for the askin'?"

Douglas' grin couldn't be suppressed as it exploded into laughter, and he spurted out, "All 826 of you!" He doubled over, once again pleased with his own humor.

I didn't find it as funny as he did, although through my growing melancholy mood, a smile snuck out. How I'd missed my dear goofy friend.

Christ simply looked on us with mild amusement, as Peggy Lee's exquisite voice surrounded us, singing her hit, "Is That All There Is?"

An unseen hand turned down the volume, allowing Douglas and me to clearly hear Christ when he asked me if I was truly that disillusioned.

An honest review of my recent history, meaning the last few years of my life, did not lend itself to an easy answer to that question.

In many ways, I had reached a point where I'd realized the best of love and family. I had become a more understanding and broader thinking and accepting person.

I also had lived to see horrible inhumanity and political injustice, causing people that I thought I knew and respected to become hateful and bigoted. This has made me sadder and more disillusioned than I could ever have imagined. Also, heath issues had been a drag. Mostly, the answer is, yeah, I'm that disillusioned. I know that I've hardly seen anything on this side. And, God knows, oh, sorry, no disrespect, I have certainly screwed things up on THAT side...

"826 times!" Douglas snapped.

"How can you screw things up? You put too much pressure on yourself... The entire human race does this to itself! It's maddening! No wonder you feel hopeless, thinking that way!" Christ said, as his furrowed brow told the story of His concern.

"How can I NOT think that way? In every frame of my life's review, there was an example of me causing pain or not living up to my abilities... I had a lifetime of it!"

"826 of 'em!" Douglas, of course, interjected.

Trying to express how serious I was, I raised my hand, as if to stop Douglas from making light of my feelings, allowing Christ a beat to interject His own thought:

"You aren't supposed to be perfect," he simply said.

His statement hung in the air for what seemed like a long time before our resident jokester broke what must have been an uncomfortable silence for him by adding, "You mean, I'm not?"

My general malaise and mild depression that accompanied me in life followed me to this transition place. I'm not suggesting that I was/am an unhappy guy, only that as my circumstances changed, so did my levels of contentment. When I fell asleep earlier this evening, I was very content. I'd had a great day! I wasn't so jaded that happy moments couldn't reach me; no, many a time those moments sustained me when the low-ebb demons would try to sneak in.

What I feel is probably what many experience as youth slips away. The battle between the experiences and wisdom gained while abilities and opportunities wane have sapped my spirit at times, I admit. Wanting to contribute more to my family now that my abilities and opportunities are limited can make me want to pull my ever-graying hair out! Yeah, I suppose it's a pretty common feeling among us newly retired or disabled types. I gotta find something to do… something to be passionate about.

In a corner of our consciousness, we knew that a siren pierced the quiet night of my suburban neighborhood.

MINUTE SIX

The awareness of the distant siren kept my attention for a beat longer than it did my old pal and my mystical new one. In that second, I thought of how I'd react to a passing ambulance, usually by saying a silent prayer for those whose lives are about to be forever changed, with added thanks to the responders. This time the emergency call was for me, and the lives to be altered were those of my loved ones. And I could see it unravel from here. It was numbing.

"That's not an important issue, believe it or not," Douglas said sternly, snapping my attention back to our conversation.

"Seems important to me, Douglas! Maybe I'm being given a chance to do things better… get my fun meter back and spread the word that fear is the cancer of life and that we should relax and enjoy life and each other more. I don't know, yet I do know that I've got to make a decision, soon. Don't I?"

"Here, 'soon' is a relative term," Christ calmly stated. "You have all the time you need to find the answer to your question."

"Which is?" I asked.

"Well, in a nutshell…" and then, in a beautiful baritone soulful voice, he sang, "'Is that all there is…"

As He finished His exquisite rendition of Peggy's song, He walked over to me and embraced me, making me feel as if I were the center of the universe.

"Is that it? Do we keep going in circles on this loop of graduated experiences until we reach Nirvana?" I asked, mostly rhetorically. "Truth is, it really doesn't matter.

I could be done with life #827 and stay here with you two right now and let Kim and Matty and anyone else who might give a damn about me mourn for a bit and then get a fresh start. Or, maybe, like I said, I'm being given a fresh start myself."

"Not unless you allow yourself to heal first, Peter. No reason to return if you really haven't found that 'passion'," Christ said, as He relaxed our embrace and simply faded from sight.

"WOW! I love this place!" Douglas nearly screamed. "We sure aren't in Kansas anymore!"

"Where'd He go! I've got a lot more that I want to ask Him. Douglas? Douglas?"

I was left on this stunning beach with my pets, so I can't say that I was alone, yet I'd never felt so alone as I did at that moment. As my beloved animals circled me and lounged, all I could focus on was the question... "Is that all there is?"

Yeah, that's it. That's all there is. If you let yourself "drift" and accept the common theory that because you are older or damaged or whatever... now it's time to drift off semi-gracefully to be the "guy that used to be" or some other BS definition of a washed-up senior citizen. Yup, that's it. I know. I've been there. After my spinal surgery, which only relieved half the pain, I spent my days, then months and into years laying around due to the pain and the effects of pain meds. Both the drugs and the inactivity became habits. Passion killing habits.

My passion had primarily been music. Primarily music, because, although I am a singer, it is the business and social aspects of music that drove my passion. I began singing as a teenager. My social world revolved around music and continued through my career, as I began producing concerts and licensing music. Long story short, as my career ended, and, social activity diminished, I let myself "drift."

I had a bunch of great reasons to buy into this mind and body set. I lost touch with prior business contacts. Many of them, as I had worked with an older demographic, had passed away. Mix in my physical difficulties and PRESTO! There you have it! A passion-less, about-to-be-has-been! I was finally waking up from this self-imposed (or accepted) nightmare. I had reduced my daily opioid usage by two-thirds over the last year. I had designed a series of shows and begun marketing them. I even started getting in shape by stretching and doing squats; I started practicing singing my scales. I was committed to working.

My pain was much better because of a nerve ablation. My biggest battle was with my energy levels; I didn't have any. Laying around for years had taken a toll on my already beat-up body, but I was determined to get back out there.

The vision of my new pal, Jesus H. Christ, singing, "Is that all there is," popped into my head, prompting a laugh. So did my next thought: when I finally got to the point that I could get back to the world, I died! To think! I used to love irony!

My internal chuckles dissipated that momentary feeling of deep loneliness. It seemed as if the mere act of laughing brought with it its meaning—love, lightness, joy, and pleasure. These impressions filled the space in me that was vacated when loneliness left with my laughter. I can only describe the experience as that of being ecstatic! As soon as my entire being was encompassed with emotions more positive than I had ever sensed before, I ceased existing as I had been. I was now simply... I'm not sure that I can communicate this, yet it's as if I evaporated into the surrounding atmosphere... like I became one with... with... everything!

I was no longer subject to the confines of my body, yet I somehow innately understood that I still had limitations, just not exactly physical. Weird.

Disembodied, and at the same time, contained to a limited, yet unseen space.

At that exact moment, the beautiful vision of my personal beach on Bali along with my pets seemed to vaporize, instantly morphing from solid to mist-like outlines that then faded into the same unseen space. This activity was both witnessed and experienced by me.

This affected me similarly to the way that I was given expanded mental capacity, yet now that I was no longer a physical being, I was flooded with a rush of goodness and love beyond description. Beyond, I imagine, what I could have contained while occupying my body. It was as if a point of light originated at my center, then immediately burst into a billion or more laser-like beams blasting throughout the galaxies. And that doesn't begin to tell the truth or the depth of the feeling and power in that love, that goodness.

I no longer felt alone. I experienced loneliness for only a split second. A very soul piercing split second.

The power in experiencing, in the next split second, the exact opposite, was clarifying.

"You don't have to be perfect," I recalled He pointedly stressed.

From this position of acceptance and love, I understood. This view of myself as a human from a place devoid of ego allowed me to see that I was doing alright on my humanity trip #827. From here, it was easy to see how hard I was being on myself as of late. Actually, this vantage point made it impossible not to see this. The only message I could glean from this thought was washed with a love that would make hippies swoon, that Douglas and Christ were both right, in their own ways: "You don't have to be perfect."

Christ, knowing that the deep, pure levels of egoless love and community are one with us, always is correct. And, for the same reason, so is Douglas, when teasingly suggesting that he is, of course, perfect. Perfect only in that moment, that action or deed. Other than that, perfection in totality is not something you might expect. That would certainly answer the question, "Is that all there is?" And what fun would that be?

This sense of being dis-embodied is oddly familiar and freeing. It gives the powerful impression of vastness and an ability to be nearly anywhere and everywhere at once, should I want or need to. For lack of words, it was god-like and wonderful.

My being, my conscience, was full of pure acceptance and oneness. I was without resistance. For that instant, I felt perfection. I felt cleaned and renewed. It was a brief respite from everything prior, unrelated, yet directly related too. This was, I suppose, Heaven—the Source.

I had been given a glimpse of this before; this sense of being dis-embodied yet one-with-all, though this time, the experience was pushed up a notch or two! My personage remained, and I recalled noticing that although I seemed to be scattered to the far corners of the universe, maybe just specs of stardust, my intellect and outlook, and yes, even my ego, were present. Only much less…judgmental. More pragmatic. Not without emotion, however. My evaluation of these changes took but a second as my attention was drawn "outward", creating a sensation of expanding the already undefined borders of my existence. This feeling of exponential growth had no relationship with anything I had yet come in contact with. There was no point of reference. Yet if I were pressed to choose a word to describe my emotions, my feelings… that word would be warmth. I was wrapped in it, floating in it. Regardless of the completely foreign place I was transported to, due to the sensation of warmth, nothing but beautiful and serene emotions flowed from and through me.

Then a slow-motion vision of me, being loaded onto a stretcher, came into view.

My sense of serenity shifted immediately. Not as dramatically as it might have before I had been granted this new vantage point, but it changed. I was shocked backed to the reality that I still had to make a decision. One that does not get easier with more information.

With my latest revelation, it appeared my "personality" survived the transition, retaining elements of my emotions, my opinions, of being Mr. #827. Though my best self-seemed to surface and survive here, my ego having been tapped down and intellect amped up, it dawned on me that should I decide to make my transition one way, so to speak, my heart may still be heavy for those that I love and leave behind. And, for those unfinished dreams and desires.

My sarcastic nature and sense of humor was also surviving this transition, as my reaction to discovering that my feelings of longing and loss that I had assumed were strictly human, were not, was to laugh. Not a cheek busting laugh nor a good belly laugh. More of a snide, sarcastic, sadly tinged laugh that had no place here. This feeling was completely out of context. My seemingly connection with the Source made me assume that such an emotional response to "earthly matters" was somehow incorrect, or immature. Then, as it had before, Source communicated in that osmosis like form, reminding me that I was still not in one place or the other. I was also told that I would always love and be connected to those who remained on earth. At the same instant, in the same thought, the individual love of those special to me, those that transitioned before and are now with Source, were made known to me. Not directly, not yet. Just conceptually; that my separate group of loved ones await me... on all planes. And that my sense of melancholy is definitely a human trait, and that the input from these emotions is what drives the evolution of Source. It also attracts the soul to reincarnation. The draw of humanity, to experience life and to love, are powerful forces. Strong enough to separate, in a way, the soul from Source.

The need, the draw to have a human experience, is both a personal one and a Source need. Individuals are drawn for a multitude of life reasons. Life lessons are as varied and distinct as we are. Yet regardless of the individual lessons to be learned and paths to be followed, they all contribute to the expansion of the whole Source, forming a perfectly symbiotic relationship.

I'm realizing, again from my sarcastic viewpoint, that I'm akin to a worker ant servicing his queen, here played by the Source. I hurry through my busy day, my life, gathering the required elements of survival and development in the physical world, in order to mature and progress my soul, all while contributing to the whole of Source. The traditional "reward" of eternal heaven has been taken from me by this blissful awareness of reality, replaced by the idea of carrying emotional baggage of one degree or another throughout an eternity of reincarnations. Well, that thought is kind of a drag. "But you're growing and learning so much, darling!" I could hear someone saying in my mind. "Yeah, yeah, yeah!" I heard myself respond, halfheartedly. Not a very good trade off. However,...

We are constantly surrounded by those that know and love us. We are never alone, although we may sometimes feel that we are. Oddly, it is only when we are in human form that we experience loneliness. It is impossible to keep souls from rejoining Source when exiting a human body, as home for the spirit is

Source. When in human form, one often finds him or herself isolated and feeling alone, rejecting the acceptance and companionship of others. Maybe it is necessary to include some degree of sadness in every human experience. Maybe. Perhaps it's the chase of the high, the bounce back from the fall that drives us, that allows us to face the failures and the pain of loss. Maybe.

I felt, too, in that moment, that being here, on this and in this unworldly plane, that all my maladies, uncertainties and even sadness would be more than addressed; they would be understood and corrected. It was that secure sense of warmth that superseded the gnawing ache I projected I would feel when leaving my family behind. That same warm sensation forecast the availability of any healing activity I may need, be it residual damage from this last physical lifetime or spiritual healing. There was comfort in this. And a sense of familiarity. It was like coming home. Not to the kind of home most of us have, crazy and dysfunctional as all get out (and I cleaned that up!), but to that idealistic one, the perfect "as seen on TV" home. Warm, comfortable and safe. Yet with challenges.

Minute Seven

I knew that if I stayed, there was work to be done. This was not a place to languish, floating amongst the puffy clouds whilst strumming one's harp. No, there was healing to be done and time to commit to understanding where my energy might be better spent next time around. I now also understood that this was true should I decide to return to my body, and apply what, if any, of this knowledge and wisdom I'd acquired during these dramatic moments to the balance of that experience.

The decision facing me was a curious one. Regardless of my choice, much work awaited me.

Having been given this wonderful gift of the view from this realm, I could clearly see how and where I could improve myself and better contribute to those in my life. My life review left me with great empathy by letting me feel every injustice I ever did to others. If I could remember the depths of this pain, if the veil would allow these memories to come through, my decision would be easier...

The timelessness of this place was appealing. It dawned on me that I may carry my sadness or discontent with me to this place, this plane, yet at least time wouldn't matter. Then darkness. Sudden, deep and complete darkness.

A single strand of light shattered the deep void. It began from a place that would seem like where I would be, if I were actually centered somewhere, and snaked outward for a long but visible distance. Colors of various intensity began to define sections of differing lengths; I didn't need to count them. I knew. Including the first and brightest of the glowing beams, there were 827.

They were joined by layer after layer of similar light strands, all now starting to gently pulsate as they intertwined. They formed a union not unlike a tightly knit garment, strand after strand woven amongst and between each other. The lifetime each shaded strand represented, and the knowledge contained therein, could be accessed simply by thought. We are all part of the whole, and each individual experience is available to any of us at any time. It boils down to being one with the Source.

Set against that blackest void, the sight was stunning. The message, equally so. To see so clearly how each of our lives are connected throughout eternity reaffirmed my belief that we are missing the boat in the way that we look at religion, politics and each other. The majestic beauty shown to me of the eternal spiritual relationship we share sure looked like heaven compared to our lives in a body. A more realistic version of heaven, from my point of view, anyway.

I generally understood our relationship to polarity. Our planet and everything under its sun operated that way. It is for that same reason I never understood that heaven, in the way that the Catholic Church presented it, would be a place anyone would want to go. How boring would eternity be, if all you could count on was another perfect experience? Without conflict, or at least the possibility of some, life, or afterlife, would seem pretty dull. I felt that way as a kid in parochial school and still did, right up to and including this moment. It appeared that I may be on to something. This peek behind the curtain was extraordinary.

The offerings of this version of "heaven" appeared to be far more stimulating than the standard one. My guess was that I could access this intricate and exact library of history, life by life, throughout the entire existence of mankind in order to find answers to questions now beyond my comprehension. I had already been shown that we communicate with Source and any other loved one at will. The deeper I went, the more I was shown, the further away fear drifts.

I know that there is nothing to fear in transitioning. I know that there is no death. I know that human love transcends time and form.

What a great way to spend eternity between trips to earth… or perhaps other planets or existences!

Yet I remained torn. My life, #827, somehow, felt unfinished. I'm not sure how it could. I didn't let much grass grow under my feet, as the saying goes. I was a jack of all trades. I didn't do it all, but I covered the work spectrum from manual labor to concert producer. I've had great friends and now have a wonderful loving mate and family. No, it's not the professional life that feels wanting. My hesitation in staying here and delving deeper into this cocoon of warmth and endless knowledge that's wrapped up in another kind of warmth. This sensation and connection are also relatively new to me, seeing as we'd been together just over nine years. Add to this the wonderful gift that is our grandson, Matty... Well, I'd never experienced anything like it, until now. Another type of heaven.

There is no question that my life has been a full one. Yet the question, I suppose, is, has it been fulfilling? Or is that the question? In the short time that I'd been here (or has it been an eternity?), the lack of judgment applied to one's lifetime decisions implies that there are no wrong choices. Each choice produces a consequence that presents another choice and so it goes, feeding Source with an endless number of experiences from which to grow. No right or wrong, just is. So, what to do, what to do? First off, I really don't buy into that "just is" philosophy. Not completely. Let's remember, at least on planet earth, where the entire deal is set up on the premise of the survival of the fittest, something's going to die if something else is going to eat. But you don't have to be cruel. So, I believe in consequences.

My thoughts were interrupted by the anxious and confused voice of my precious grandson. He was reacting to the EMTs securing my still lifeless body on the stretcher as he called, "Poppa, wake up, poppa, wake up!"

I watched as he clung to Kim's leg and cried. She knelt down to hug and comfort him and whispered that everything was going to be alright.

"Have no fear," she said.

Wise woman, she is.

From my unique perch, both galaxies away and right next to them, I felt their experience, the deep sadness, confusion and sense of helplessness. Kim was rightfully focusing on Matty, yet as always, she was shouldering the load for everyone. She would see to it that the best would be made of this situation, regardless of the outcome. This is an example of the quiet, committed, unassuming love Kim brings to our lives. She truly is a wonderful person.

Ah, yes. The outcome. It may seem odd that the choice between living out the balance of life #827 or accepting the more than generous offer to stay here, in this "heavenly" place, is a difficult one, yet it is. The more I am made privy to on my "galactical tour among the gods", the more I'm starting to think it's so connected, so intertwined with earthbound experiences, that whether I stay or not, it makes no difference. The choice matters none to Source," it matters only to me.

Another thought dawned on me. Being solely in the spiritual plane, I think I would be viewing everything from a completely different perspective. Here, there are no physical reactions or responses; only cerebral, mental, spiritual, call it what you will... The thought made me feel momentarily untethered from those "warm feelings" that had moments ago enveloped me, and once again, I felt uncertain and heartsick. I wondered if I would lose my capacity to love along with my body and become more analytical. I feared that with the suppression of ego and emotion, the spiritual side was starting to feel that way to me.

A fabulous vision of the colorful library of all knowledge vibrantly pulsed before and around me, seemingly to remind me that I could access the experiences of any lifetime, oddly causing me to think that at least I could peer in on other's emotional experiences, turning me into an eternal voyeur of sorts. Or would I even care? Again, my thoughts were starting to spin out of control. My human nature surged to the forefront, bringing this confusion to the otherwise peaceful realm of this bizarre transitional place.

My new pal, Jesus H. Christ, calmed me down last time my thoughts were heading this way... He just reached over and touched me, and my thoughts were calmed. As I was thinking that I sure could use a friend like that again right now, He called to me, seemingly from quite a distance, asking, "What are you doing to yourself? Remember... think of when you were most happy."

I turned in the direction of where I thought His voice had come from, only to find myself back on that beautiful beach in Bali. My excited pets were gone, as was Douglas. Christ, whose voice had obviously led me here, was nowhere in sight. I stood and tried to absorb everything around me, the sights and sounds, scents and sensations. I was alone, yet the combination of being again on this idyllic beach and having heard from my new pal, put me back in control of my thoughts. I calmed down.

I walked along the edge of the surf line vaguely in search of Douglas or Jesus. What I was truly seeking was my answer while simultaneously avoiding the question, can I recapture my passion? Hell, can I even recall what it feels like?

Lifetime #827's successful completion hinged on the answer. Time was running out, if I was going to choose not to stay.

The warm surf swirling around my feet pleasantly distracted my thoughts, rerouting them back to a wonderful time when, as a younger man, I approached my life fearlessly. I wasn't concerned with other's opinions of me, or what I might earn on a particular project; I followed my instincts. I did what felt correct. I admit that I wasn't always successful yet being considerate of all parties became a priority. Clearly seeing the end result was also a priority. Approaching and following the path to that goal fearlessly was a priority.

As I shuffled through the soothing sea foam, I saw clearly that the key to the wonderful memories of those more youthful times was my tunnel vision and confident approach towards my life and goals.

And there it was. As if the entire world, or wherever I was in this ever-expanding universe, stopped, and as clearly as I could ever hope to see, there was my answer. It was so simple. Whenever I allowed myself to move freely through life, untethered from fear of failure or rejection, I was happy. Looking back, those were times when I was tuned in, doing things correctly.

It was with childlike wonder and enthusiasm that I would greet those days, eager to meet the people and situations and opportunities that were waiting for me. I expected to find such people and opportunities... and find I did.

Recalling how I felt during the many times that I experienced this mindset throughout my life, as well as those when I had lost touch with my fearlessness, cemented the truth behind the belief that heaven is everywhere that fear is not.

The ebbing foam of the warm sea at my feet reminded me that I wasn't home. I wasn't standing on a beach on Earth, no. I was somewhere in between— in transition. I had been given a rare opportunity to choose between returning to my life and finishing my life differently with the knowledge I was gifted during this experience, or simply choose to stay. Regarding this, there seemed to be no wrong answer.

Yet this too was an illusion. Now that I had been armed with the knowledge, the incredibly simple fact that fear is the basis of all disfunction, control and disease, I was not left with a choice. I was left with a responsibility to, in whatever way that I could, share the importance of this simple yet powerful truth: fear is our enemy, and beyond the benefit of fight or flight, fear has no place in our lives.

The split second it took for me to process this revelation was equivalent to the time it took for my spirit to travel from that pristine and peaceful beach back to my heretofore lifeless body.

The merging of body and spirit created a violent reaction. I gasped and convulsed in pain, jerking to a half sitting position. The EMTs steadied me as I nearly toppled the gurney, which was near the rear of the ambulance sitting on uneven ground. Everyone was extremely surprised. The medical staff had presumably written me off, seeing as I had been unresponsive for more than seven minutes, while my family had been holding on to whatever hope they could.

I am, once again, wide-eyed and childlike in my fearless approach to my future. My hope is that all who hear the message of the gift that was given to me during my transition will realize that fear is what takes the joy from your life. There is nothing to fear. Simply be kind and love. Always.

Epilogue

Wake up! You're having a nightmare!" Kim whispered into my ear as she gently shook me.

"No, not a bad dream. More real than that, more important…" I softly responded.

And then I realized that what had just happened was so much more than a dream. It felt as if it were a message meant to be shared. A loving call to really wake up. To wake up from the distractions and disease that fear brings. *Wake Up.*

Made in United States
North Haven, CT
04 July 2024